# the CRitteR club

**#5**

## Amy Meets Her Stepsister

**#6**

## Ellie's Lovely Idea

**#7**

## Liz at Marigold Lake

**#8**

## Marion Strikes a Pose

by Callie Barkley ♥ illustrated by Marsha Riti

LITTLE SIMON

New York   London   Toronto   Sydney   New Delhi

LITTLE SIMON

An imprint of Simon & Schuster Children's Publishing Division • 1230 Avenue of the Americas, New York, New York 10020 • This Little Simon bind-up edition March 2016. • *Amy Meets Her Stepsister, Ellie's Lovely Idea,* and *Liz at Marigold Lake* copyright © 2013 by Simon & Schuster, Inc. *Marion Strikes a Pose* copyright © 2014 by Simon & Schuster, Inc. All rights reserved, including the right of reproduction in whole or in part in any form. LITTLE SIMON is a registered trademark of Simon & Schuster, Inc., and associated colophon is a trademark of Simon & Schuster, Inc. For information about special discounts for bulk purchases, please contact Simon & Schuster Special Sales at 1-866-506-1949 or business@simonandschuster.com. The Simon & Schuster Speakers Bureau can bring authors to your live event. For more information or to book an event contact the Simon & Schuster Speakers Bureau at 1-866-248-3049 or visit our website at www.simonspeakers.com.

Designed by Laura Roode

The text of this book was set in ITC Stone Informal Std.

Manufactured in the United States of America 0216 FFG

10 9 8 7 6 5 4 3 2 1

Library of Congress Control Number 2015959774

ISBN 978-1-4814-7602-7

ISBN 978-1-4424-8217-3 (*Amy Meets Her Stepsister* eBook)

ISBN 978-1-4424-8220-3 (*Ellie's Lovely Idea* eBook)

ISBN 978-1-4424-9527-2 (*Liz at Marigold Lake* eBook)

ISBN 978-1-4424-9530-2 (*Marion Strikes a Pose* eBook)

These titles were previously published individually in hardcover and paperback by Little Simon.

# Table of Contents

# the CRitteR club

## Amy Meets Her Stepsister

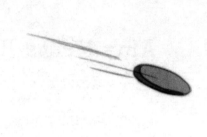

# Table of Contents

# Chapter 1

# Big, Exciting News!

Amy Purvis's mom grabbed a potholder. She lifted the pot lid. Amy took a sniff.

"Mmmm," Amy said. "That smells *so* good!"

Inside the pot was a big batch of their famous chicken noodle soup. They had made it together. "The perfect dinner for a cool night,"

Amy's mom said with a smile.

Amy giggled. "Mom, this batch will last us all year!" It *was* a lot of soup for just the two of them.

Amy set the table. She put out two napkins and two soup spoons. Meanwhile, Amy's mom ladled soup into bowls.

Just as they sat down to eat, the phone rang.

"Start without me!" said Amy's mom, popping up to answer it.

Amy slurped up some broth and noodles. Right away, she felt warm all over.

"Oh, hi, Eliot!" she heard her mom say into the phone.

Amy's face lit up. Eliot was her father. He lived in Orange Blossom, a big town near Santa Vista. Even though her parents were divorced,

Amy got to see her dad a lot.

"Uh-huh," her mom was saying into the phone. "I bet she would love that!" She looked over at Amy and smiled. "Why don't you ask her?" Her mom held out the phone to Amy. "Your dad has a question for you," she said.

Amy jumped up and took the phone.

"Hi, Dad!" she said excitedly. "What's up?"

"Hey, kiddo," came her dad's voice through the phone. "How would you like to spend this week-end at my house?"

"Really?" said Amy. She loved her weekends with her dad. "But I thought that was *next* weekend."

"I know," her dad said. "But I've got some really big and exciting news to tell you."

*News?* "What is it?" Amy asked.

"You know what? I want to tell you in person," her dad said. "Oh! And Julia is going to come visit on Saturday too."

Julia was Amy's dad's girlfriend. He had met her about a year ago. Amy really liked Julia. She still kind of wished her mom and dad were married. But since *they* didn't want that, Amy was happy her dad had

met someone as nice as Julia.

"So I'll pick you up tomorrow. Okay?" her dad said.

"Okay! Bye!" said Amy, and she hung up the phone. She was so glad she wouldn't have to wait too long for the weekend. Tomorrow was Friday!

Then it hit her. *Friday*. It was sleepover night with her three best friends: Marion, Ellie, and Liz. They had one almost every week.

With a pang of disappointment, Amy flopped down into her

chair. "Oh, no. This means I can't go to the sleepover at Marion's."

Amy's mom patted her on the back. "You'll have fun with your dad, sweetie. And when we host

next week's sleepover, we can make it extra special."

Amy nodded. *And besides,* she thought, *we have lots of sleepovers. But how often does Dad have big, exciting news?*

Now she was really curious. What *was* the big news?

19

# A Lunchtime Mystery

Amy couldn't wait for school the next day. She wanted to tell her friends about her weekend with her dad—and the mystery news! Lunchtime was their first chance to talk.

"Maybe your dad is going to run for president!" Ellie said excitedly. Her brown eyes twinkled. "Or he is going to Hollywood to be in movies! Or he found out you're related to the Queen of England!"

Amy giggled. Ellie just loved the idea of being famous!

Marion slurped the last of her

chocolate milk. "Maybe he will take you on a shopping spree!" she suggested.

Then Liz spoke up. "Maybe your dad wants to write about The Critter Club in his newspaper!"

*Hmmm . . .* , thought Amy. That was a possibility. Amy's dad was the editor of a newspaper called *The Coastal County Courier.* He knew all about The Critter Club. It was the animal shelter that the girls ran in their friend Ms. Sullivan's barn.

"That could be it," said Amy. "My dad did say one time that it would make a good story—how the club got started."

And it actually *was* a good story. Before the four girls really knew Ms. Marge Sullivan, they had helped her find her missing

The Coastal County Courier

Critter Club Helping Neighborhood Critters

puppy, Rufus. Then Ms. Sullivan had a great idea. She decided Santa Vista needed an animal shelter to help lost and stray animals. Ms. Sullivan had an empty barn, and the girls had a love of animals, and that's how it all began!

The Critte Club

It helped that Amy's mom was a veterinarian. Dr. Purvis taught the girls how to take care of the different animals that had been at The Critter Club so far: bunnies, kittens, dogs— even a turtle and a tarantula!

"Well, I am sorry I won't be around this weekend," Amy said. "I wanted to help out with the eggs."

They were incubating a dozen chicken eggs at The Critter Club.

A local farmer had dropped them off a week before. His family had to move. They had sold or given away most of their farm animals.

Then, before their move, their best hen had laid a clutch of eggs. But she didn't want to sit on them. Amy's mom said sometimes hens did that.

Luckily, the farmer knew about The Critter Club. He had brought the eggs and the incubator. The

girls were so excited to help them hatch. Then they would find the chicks new homes!

"Don't worry," said Liz. "We can handle the eggs. They're not due to hatch for another week."

"But we will miss you at the sleepover tonight!" Marion said. She put an arm around Amy's shoulders.

"Oooh! And call one of us when you get the good news!" Ellie begged. "I can't wait to hear it!"

31

# Chapter 3

# Dinner with Dad

The drive from Amy's house to her dad's only took about twenty minutes. But in that time, Amy had asked him the same question ten times.

"*Now* can you tell me the big, exciting news?" she asked again. They were pulling into his driveway.

Her dad shook his head for the

eleventh time. "Nope! You'll have to wait until dinner!" he said. "First let's get you settled in. Then we're going out."

*We're going out to dinner?* Amy thought. *This* is *a big deal.*

Amy walked into her dad's house, thinking once again how cool it was. The walls were painted bright colors. The furniture was simple and square. Her dad said the style was called "modern." His house

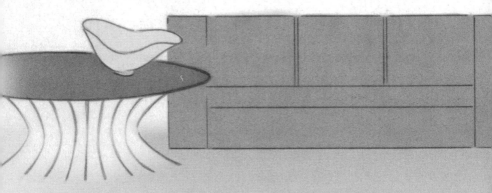

was so different from her mom's house, which was very cozy but not as colorful.

The art on her dad's walls was also really bright. *I've got to bring*

*Liz here sometime,* Amy thought.
Liz was an amazing artist. *Maybe
she can tell me what these are.*

Amy loved that she had her very
own room at her dad's house. She
plopped her heavy backpack down

on her bed. Then she unpacked. She had a huge pile of books. She had brought the newest Nancy Drew mystery, plus *The Wind in the Willows, Black Beauty,* and *The Wonderful Wizard of Oz.*

"Hungry?" her dad asked as he poked his head into Amy's room.

Amy nodded.

So off they went to dinner. It was a short walk to Amy's favorite restaurant in Orange Blossom— The Library. The walls were wall-papered with old book pages. The menu was Amy's favorite part.

The Library

Starter: The Secret Garden Salad

Appetizer: The Mad Hatter's Tea Sandwiches

Entree: 20,000 Leagues Under the Seafood Sampler

Amy and her dad ordered. When the waiter had gone, her dad smiled across the table.

"I have a pile of old newspapers we can cut up," he told her.

"Cool!" Amy exclaimed.

Amy and her dad loved creating poems together. They cut words out of newspapers or magazines. They moved them around until they had a poem they liked.

Then they glued the words to a piece of paper.

"And, hey! What's going on with The Critter Club?" her dad went on.

Amy told him all about the eggs that were going to hatch. But she really wanted to talk about something else.

"Dad, wasn't there some big news?" Amy said. She looked at him and squinted. "It's dinnertime. Can you tell me *now*?"

Her dad smiled. "Okay, you're

right," he said. "Well, Julia is going to come over tomorrow."

"Right," said Amy. "You told me on the phone." She and her dad and Julia always had fun together.

"And Julia's going to bring some-one with her," her dad went on. "Do you remember that Julia has a daughter? Her name is Chloe."

Amy nodded. She remembered. Julia talked about Chloe a lot. Amy had never met her because Chloe was often away visiting her dad in Arizona. Amy felt the slightest flutter of butterflies in her stomach. Amy was shy about meeting new people. *But Julia is nice*, she thought. *I bet Chloe will be nice too.*

"She's eight years old, just like you are!" her dad continued.

"And . . . here's the really big news: the reason we'd love you and Chloe to finally meet is that Julia and I are engaged!"

*Engaged?* Amy's face flushed a little. "Like, getting married?" she asked.

Her dad nodded. "That's the idea," he said. "We haven't set a date yet. But we'd like to get married someday—maybe next year."

"Oh," was all Amy could think of to say. Her mind was racing. *If Dad and Julia get married, will Julia be my stepmom? And what about Chloe? Will she be my . . . stepsister?*

Now there were a million butterflies in Amy's stomach. They were fluttering around like crazy. She was really nervous about meeting Chloe.

*What if we don't have anything in*

*common?* Amy thought. *What if I don't like her? Or worse: what if she doesn't like me?*

# Chapter 4

# Chloe

The next morning, Amy woke up to the smell of pancakes. *Yum!* She got out of bed and put on her slippers. As she did, she remembered part of a dream she'd had. In it, she had been getting ready for a big fancy ball. Her dress was perfect. She was all set to leave. Then three mean stepsisters appeared and tore her beautiful dress to shreds.

*Stepsisters*, Amy thought. *I guess I really am nervous about meeting Chloe!*

Down in the kitchen, her dad was flipping pancakes. There was a place set at the table for Amy. Next to it was a stack of newspapers.

"Breakfast, coming right up!" her dad said. "Have a seat. I wrote you a poem."

Amy found the paper on the table, next to her fork.

MAYBE pigs **fly** moo *
And maybe birds
But there is no way
SOMEONE won't Like **you** .

Amy giggled. "Thanks, Dad," she said. It was like he could read her mind.

Her dad came over and gave her a kiss on the head. "Don't worry," he said. "You and Chloe will get along great."

Amy had two pancakes—then one more. She and her dad cut and pasted some poems together.

Then Amy went to her room to get dressed.

As she put on her shoes, she heard the doorbell. *Ding-dong!*

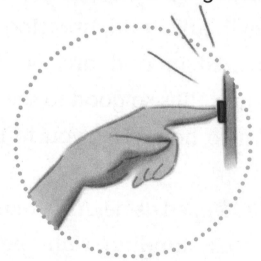

Amy took a deep breath. Then she walked toward the front hall.

Her dad was already at the door. At first, Amy could only see Julia on the front stoop. She looked the same as Amy remembered: shiny, straight black hair, sparkling brown eyes, and a big, friendly smile.

"Amy!" Julia said, spotting her. She breezed in and greeted Amy with a hug. "It's so good to see you. And I'm so happy for you to meet Chloe."

Julia stepped aside. Amy realized Chloe was standing right behind Julia. In fact, Chloe was holding on to the back of Julia's blue coat. Then, quickly, Chloe let go. She smiled at Amy.

53

Amy's first thought was: *She looks so much like her mom!* Chloe had the same shiny dark hair, but hers was in braids.

Her second thought was: *Ellie would love that outfit.* She had on a dark green dress and shiny black patent leather shoes. It reminded Amy of the pretty costumes Ellie liked to wear.

"Hi," said Chloe with a small wave.

"Nice to meet you," Amy said—
and tried hard not to blush. It happened every time Amy felt shy or
embarrassed. And at that moment,
she was feeling both.

# A Messy Beginning

Julia held up a plastic container. "It's not too early for cookies, is it?" she asked, smiling. "I was hoping you girls could help me by decorating them."

Amy thought that sounded fun!

Amy's dad set the girls up at the kitchen table. Julia had made sugar cookies that were shaped like hearts and stars. There were tubes of icing, sprinkles, and colored sugar. Julia put out a glass of water.

"For smoothing the icing," she explained.

Chloe sat down. Amy took the seat across from her.

"Julia and I are going to do some gardening out back," Amy's dad told the girls.

"Just give us a call if you need

us. Okay?" added Julia.

Chloe smiled at her mom. Amy nodded and took a cookie. Chloe did too.

Then, as their parents went out the back door, both girls reached for the tube of yellow icing.

"Oh!" said Amy. "It's okay. You take it. I'll use the blue."

Chloe didn't say anything. She just took the yellow. Then she scooted her chair a little farther from the table.

*Why did she do that?* Amy wondered. *Maybe she just needs more room to decorate. . . .*

She glanced over at Chloe. Chloe had her eyes locked on her cookie. For a few minutes, the kitchen was silent.

*Is it possible?* thought Amy. *Someone who's even shyer than I am?*

As shy as she was herself, Amy wanted to be a good hostess. "So, what school do you go to?" she asked Chloe.

At first, Chloe didn't answer. She was still staring at her cookie, squeezing out the yellow icing. But then she blurted out: "Orange Blossom School for Girls."

"Oh," said Amy. "I know where that is." She waited to see if Chloe had more to say.

She didn't.

So Amy said, "I go to Santa Vista Elementary."

Chloe didn't look up.

"My three best friends and I started an animal shelter," Amy went on. "It's called The Critter Club. We take care of strays and lost or hurt animals."

Chloe still didn't say anything.

"Do you like animals?" Amy tried.

For the first time since their parents had left, Chloe looked up. "*Ew*," she said. Her face scrunched up, like she smelled something gross. "Animals are dirty and smelly. Why would you want to be around them so much?"

Amy felt her cheeks flush hot. She had no idea what to say to that.

Just then, Chloe reached for the pink icing. Her elbow knocked over the water glass. Water spilled onto the cookie plate, soaking the cookies.

Quickly Amy reached for a towel. "Oh, don't worry," Amy said. "It's not a big deal."

Then Amy's dad walked in the back door. "Forgot my gardening gloves," he said with a smile. "How's it going?"

Chloe jumped out of her seat. She pointed at Amy. "*She* did it!" Chloe shouted. "She knocked over the water! The cookies are ruined!"

# Chapter 6

# Fashion Disaster!

Julia and Chloe cleaned up the cookies while Amy helped her dad pull some weeds in the garden.

"Hey, is everything okay, kiddo?" Amy's dad asked her. "You're being awfully quiet."

Amy nodded. But everything *wasn't* okay. *Chloe really doesn't like me,* Amy thought. *Why else would she say* I *spilled the water?*

"Okay, change of plans!" Julia said, walking outside. Chloe was behind her. "Amy, Chloe and I were talking. How about we three girls go shopping?"

Amy looked at her dad. She gave him her

*I-hate-to-shop* face. He gave her his *Oh-come-on-it-might-be-fun* face.

"I'll meet you all at the park afterward," her dad said.

"There's a great new bookstore in town," Julia went on. "We could walk there."

"Yeah!" said Chloe. She was smiling. "That's right next to *my* favorite store. We could go to both!"

"Oh!" said Amy. Shopping for books? That *was* fun. *And it kind of seems like Chloe wants me to come.*

"Okay," Amy said. She smiled back at Chloe.

*Maybe I was wrong. Maybe she doesn't hate me, after all.*

They went to Chloe's favorite store first. It was a clothing store called Threads. As soon as they stepped inside, Chloe disappeared in the clothing racks. Julia waved to the lady at the register. They seemed to know each other. Julia went over to chat.

Amy was left alone. She felt like she was frozen in her spot. It was the

kind of store that made her feel . . . lost. Minutes crept by.

Then Chloe came rushing over. She already had an armload of clothes. "Amy! Come on! Let's try some things on," Chloe said.

"No, that's okay. You can go ahead—" Amy started to say.

But Chloe grabbed her hand. She

pulled Amy to the back of the store. "Look! These would look *so, so good* on you!" Chloe said.

She handed Amy some items on hangers. Then she shooed Amy into a dressing room. "I'll try some things on next door," said Chloe. "Meet out by the mirror in five!"

Before Amy knew it, the door was closed.

Amy sighed. She really didn't

like trying things on in stores! But Chloe was being so nice. How could she say no?

So Amy put on the clothing. She looked at herself in the mirror. *This can't be right,* she thought. *I've heard of mixing patterns like stripes and polka dots. But this is ridiculous. Isn't it?*

Amy thought about Liz. Her clothes were colorful and different—and she always got compliments on her outfits. So maybe Amy looked okay, after all.

Amy took a deep breath and opened the door. Chloe was standing by the mirror. She was wearing a daisy yellow party dress, purple ballet flats, and a sparkly headband. Her outfit was so pretty!

Amy walked over and stood next

to Chloe. They both looked in the mirror.

In a flash, Amy knew: her outfit was crazy with a capital C.

Then her eyes met Chloe's in the mirror. Amy could see it in Chloe's eyes. *She's trying not to laugh!*

Chloe had made her dress up like a fool.

"Oh, my," said a saleswoman, coming over to Amy. "Dear, *what* are you wearing?"

Amy ran back into the dressing room and closed the door.

# Amy to the Rescue

The trip to the bookstore wasn't much fun either.

At least *Julia* was being nice to Amy, as always. Julia showed Amy her favorite books from when she was a girl. Amy thought she'd like to read some of them.

Then Julia headed to the cook-book section. Chloe came over. "Hey,

Amy," she said. "Have you read these?" She held out a small pile of books. Amy reached out to take them.

Chloe let go before Amy had a grip. The books fell to the floor. *Thwump!* Other shoppers nearby turned to look. Amy's face flushed.

Was it just Amy's imagination, or had Chloe done that on purpose?

In the bookstore café, Julia got each girl a hot chocolate. While Julia paid, Amy headed to the counter. She reached for the cinnamon.

"Oh, I love cinnamon too!" said Chloe, appearing at Amy's side. She snatched up the cinnamon. "Here, let me!" She started sprinkling the cinnamon on Amy's hot chocolate.

"Thanks!" said Amy.

Chloe kept sprinkling.

"Okay!" Amy said. "That's great."

Chloe kept sprinkling.

"Chloe! That's enough!" Amy covered the top of her cup. Chloe finally stopped.

Amy sipped her hot chocolate. It was *way* too cinnamon-y.

Amy was glad when they met her dad in the park. He had brought a picnic for them.

"How was the shopping?" he asked Amy. They were tossing the Frisbee. Chloe and Julia were sitting together over on the picnic blanket.

Amy shrugged. "It—it was okay," she said glumly.

She had thought it would be such a fun weekend. But now she just missed Liz, Ellie, and Marion.

"Call us when you get the good news!" Ellie had said. Turned out it wasn't good news at all. Amy had a wicked stepsister!

Amy threw the Frisbee. The wind blew it a little off course. It glided toward the picnic blanket.

Out of nowhere, a dog came

running out of some bushes. It was chasing the Frisbee and barking like crazy.

Chloe saw the dog coming her way—and let out an ear-piercing scream! She jumped up and darted behind Julia.

Meanwhile, the Frisbee landed next to the blanket. The dog, a Dalmatian, ran right past it. Now the dog was more interested in Chloe! It ran up to her and barked.

Chloe screamed again and ran behind a tree.

The dog chased her, barking and wagging its tail.

Chloe needed help. Amy ran over. "Chloe," she said calmly. "It's okay." Chloe looked terrified. "Trust me," Amy said. Then she turned to face the dog. The two girls stood side by side.

"Sit!" Amy said firmly.

The dog stopped barking and froze. Then it sat back on its hind legs.

"Stay!" Amy said.

The dog sat very still, watching Amy. It seemed to be waiting for another command.

Chloe turned to Amy. "Thank you!" she cried, and hugged her tight.

# A New Friend?

"Nice going, kiddo," Amy's dad said, and patted her on the back.

Julia had an arm around Chloe, who still looked shaken up. "That was amazing," Julia said. "Thank you, Amy. Chloe is sometimes a little scared of animals."

Amy remembered what Chloe had said earlier about animals

being smelly and dirty. *Maybe she just didn't want to say she was afraid of them.*

"My mom has had Dalmatians at her vet clinic," Amy explained. "She told me that they have a lot of energy and are

very playful. I think this dog just wanted to play with Chloe."

The dog—who was female—was still sitting quietly. She watched them talking.

"She doesn't have a collar or a tag," Amy noticed.

Amy's dad looked around. "I wonder if she got loose from her owner," he said.

Together, they walked around the park. They didn't see anyone who seemed to be looking for a dog.

Luckily, the Orange Blossom Animal Shelter was only two blocks away. They decided to take the dog over there. "We can see if anyone has reported her missing," Julia said.

They packed up their picnic basket. As they walked toward the shelter, the dog followed closely behind Amy. Chloe cautiously came up to walk by Amy's side.

"Thanks again, Amy," she said quietly. "You really helped me out."

"It was no problem," Amy said. "Really."

They walked along without talking for a minute. Then Chloe said, "I *was* listening before when you told me about The Critter Club. And that you started it with your three best friends. I have three best friends too. We have a jewelry-making club called the Sapphire Society."

"Cool!" said Amy. "That sounds fun!" She really meant it.

Chloe nodded. "And my mom says you like mysteries?"

Amy beamed. "I wouldn't go anywhere without a Nancy Drew," she told Chloe.

"Me too!" said Chloe.

*Wow*, thought Amy. *Maybe we do have some stuff in common.*

When they got to the Orange Blossom Animal Shelter, they led the dog inside. At the front desk, they met the owner, Mr. Beebe.

"Ah, yes," Mr. Beebe said. "The Dalmatian. I've been getting calls about you, young lady," he said to the dog.

The dog barked once, as if she understood. "I've heard she's been roaming around town for about a week now. We put up some flyers with her description. But we haven't

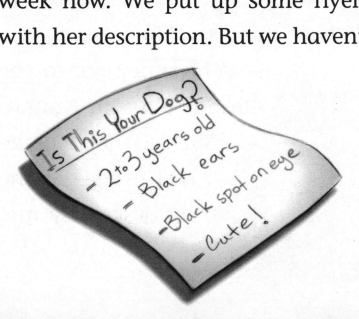

gotten a call from anyone looking for her," Mr. Beebe continued. "She must be a stray."

"Poor girl," said Julia, petting the dog's head. "She seems like she'd make a great pet for someone. What can we do to help her?"

Mr. Beebe sighed. "The problem is, we're pretty crowded right now," he said. "We have so many animals we need to find homes for. I don't suppose you folks know anyone who might be able to find her a good home?"

Amy smiled at her dad. Amy's dad smiled back.

"Mr. Beebe," said Amy, "I know just the place."

A look of understanding brightened Chloe's face. "The Critter Club!" she exclaimed.

# Heart-to-Heart

That evening back at the house, Amy, her dad, Chloe, and Julia were playing a board game.

"It was nice of Mr. Beebe to let Penny stay over tonight at the shelter," said Amy. Penny was the name they'd given the Dalmatian.

Amy's dad nodded. "And it was nice of your mom to agree to pick

105

Penny up tomorrow when she comes to get you," he said.

Dr. Purvis was even going to give the dog a checkup at her clinic. She wanted to make sure Penny was healthy before they took her to The Critter Club.

"How about some cookies for dessert?" Julia said.

"Yum!" cried Amy and Chloe together. They both laughed.

Amy's dad and Julia went to get the cookies. Chloe rolled the dice.

"You know what?" Chloe said. "I thought of one other thing we have in common."

"What?" said Amy.

"We're both only children," said Chloe. She moved her game piece. "I've always wanted a sister. But when my mom told me that she and your dad were going to get married . . . I don't know. I guess I started to worry about it. I was *super* nervous to meet you."

"Really?" said Amy. "To meet *me*?"

Chloe nodded. "I'm sorry for the way I acted," she said to Amy.

Amy smiled. "That's okay," she told Chloe. "I was really nervous

too. I was scared you wouldn't like me." Her cheeks flushed a little. "And then I was *sure* you didn't."

Chloe shook her head. "No, I just kept messing up! All day! I blamed you for spilling the water because, well, I didn't  want your dad to be mad at me. I just really want him to like me. And at the clothing store, I was trying to be silly, not mean. But then I could tell you were upset and . . . I didn't know what to say."

Amy laughed.

Chloe also explained that she had tripped at the bookstore and accidentally dropped the books. And she hadn't been paying attention with the cinnamon. Chloe looked down. "I'm sorry I messed up your hot chocolate."

"It's really okay," Amy said. She felt so relieved. Her future stepsister wasn't mean, after all. "I guess we

act nervous in different ways. My face turns bright red. You do crazy stuff!"

Amy and Chloe giggled together. Then Amy had an idea.

"You have to come visit me in Santa Vista sometime!" she told Chloe. "I'll take you to The Critter

Club. We have some chicks that are going to hatch soon."

Chloe looked like she was thinking it over. "Chicks?" she said. "You mean like tiny, yellow, fluffy baby chickens?"

Amy nodded. "Yep. They don't bark at all!"

Chloe smiled. "That sounds great. You've got a deal."

# *More* Big, Exciting News

On Sunday, Marion, Ellie, and Liz met Amy at The Critter Club. Amy and her mom had brought Penny over that morning. She seemed to be settling right in. She was already best friends with Rufus, Ms. Sullivan's dog. They ran and played together while Amy told her friends about the weekend. There was so much to tell: about finding Penny, about her dad getting engaged, and all about Chloe!

"You guys will like her a lot," Amy said. "She likes pretty clothes and jewelry—just like you, Marion." Marion smiled. "She decorated her cookies with lots of cool designs— like you would, Liz."

"I like her already!" said Liz.

"And she really loves sparkles!" added Amy.

"Like me!" exclaimed Ellie. She twirled around in her sparkly dress. The girls giggled.

"Well, I'm excited to meet her," Marion said. "And I'm glad you're back, Amy."

"Yeah!" said Liz. "We missed you. *And* it's about to get pretty busy around here. Come see!"

She pulled Amy toward the egg incubator inside the barn. Amy gasped. There was a teeny, tiny beak poking out of a hole in one of the eggs.

"Surprise!" Ellie said.

"It started hatching yesterday," said Marion, "ahead of schedule."

"The others can't be far behind!" Liz added.

Amy clapped. "Amazing!" she exclaimed. She looked at the little chick peeking out at them. "You're the very first one! But your new brothers and sisters could hatch any minute now!"

Then Amy leaned in closer. She whispered something only the chick could hear: "Don't be nervous. I'm sure you guys will get along great."

# the CRitteR club

## :paw: Ellie's Lovely Idea :paw:

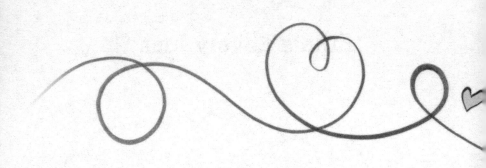

# Table of Contents

# Chapter 1

# Love Is in the Air

Early on a Saturday morning, Ellie and her three best friends, Liz, Marion, and Amy, were making valentines in Amy's kitchen. The girls had slept over at Amy's house. They were still in their pajamas!

"Ten down, ten to go!" Ellie said, adding a valentine to her DONE pile. She smiled. Ellie loved seeing her name in red glitter!

Valentine's Day was next Friday— less than a week away! There would

a party in their second-grade class. The girls were making valentines to give to their classmates.

"Valentine's Day is so much

fun," said Liz as she finished up her second valentine. Liz was a true artist. She was taking lots of time on each card.

"Me too," Marion said. "February would be so boring without it." Marion was using lots of ribbon.

Each one of her cards looked like an award. Marion knew all about winning awards. She was really good at piano and ballet and a great horseback rider.

"It *has* been a quiet month," said Amy. She was cutting and folding her cards into tiny books. "We haven't had any animals at the Critter Club for weeks!"

The Critter Club was the animal shelter that the four girls had started in their town of Santa Vista. Their friend Ms. Sullivan had come up with the idea after the girls had found her missing puppy. Ms. Sullivan had even let them take over her empty barn. Now it was the Critter Club! With the help of Amy's mom, who was

a veterinarian, the girls cared for stray, lost, or hurt animals.

"That reminds me!" cried Amy. "We got a photo from the woman who adopted Penny." Penny was a stray Dalmatian that the girls had been taking care of—until a few weeks ago. Together they had found the perfect home for her.

Amy got the photo from the kitchen.

Ellie sighed. "I sure do miss having her around the Critter Club." Amy, Liz, and Marion all nodded.

Just then, Amy's mom, Dr. Purvis, came in from the living room. "I couldn't help overhearing you girls while I was opening the mail," she said. "You know, just because there are no animals at the club doesn't mean you can't help some *other* animals."

Dr. Purvis dropped an open envelope onto the table. Then she winked and walked away.

Ellie reached for the envelope. She pulled out the paper inside. Amy, Liz, and

Show your Love
♥ for ♥
PUPPY
L♥VE!

HELP US HELP PUPPIES!

Marion looked over her shoulder.

"Oh! Puppy Love!" said Amy. "This is an organization that my mom's friend Rebecca started. That's her." Amy pointed to the woman in the photo. "She gives money to families who need help paying for their new puppy's

medical care—like all the shots that keep a puppy healthy."

"It looks like Puppy Love is try- ing to raise more money," Marion pointed out.

Ellie looked at the cute puppies in the photo and smiled. *How much* money do I have at home in my piggy bank? she wondered. *Twelve dollars?* She would gladly donate it all to Puppy Love to help those families— and puppies—who needed it.

*I just wish it could be more,* she thought. *Much, much more.*

# chapter 2

# A Musical Idea

Ellie and her nana Gloria carried bowls of popcorn into the family room. It was Saturday night—movie night—at Ellie's house. But her parents had gone out to dinner and her little brother, Toby, was upstairs reading.

"Guess it's just us tonight, Nana," Ellie said with a smile. Watching

old movies with her grandmother was one of her
favorite things to do.

"Just us! Just
us!" squawked
Lenny the parrot
from his perch in the
corner. Lenny belonged
to Nana Gloria. Together
they had come to live
with Ellie's family.

Ellie laughed. "You too, Lenny!"

"What movie are we watching
tonight?" Nana Gloria asked.

"Ms. Sullivan lent it to me,"

Ellie said. "It's called *The Singing Telegram*. And the star of it is Ruby Fairchild—your favorite!"

As Nana Gloria clapped, Ellie smiled a secret smile. She was the only one who knew that Ms. Sullivan had once been known as the famous Hollywood actress Ruby Fairchild.

That was years and years ago. Now Ms. Sullivan wanted to have a quiet life in Santa Vista. Her secret was safe with Ellie.

Ellie sat next to Nana Gloria and pressed play on the remote.

Like all of Ruby Fairchild's movies, this one was black and white.

The movie was about a shy young man who falls in love with a young woman. The only time he feels

sure of himself is when he is sing-ing. So he gets a job as a telegram deliveryman. One day he delivers a singing telegram to the woman he

loves, telling her of his feelings. But he doesn't say who it's from. By the end of the movie, she figures it out and they live happily ever after.

Ellie loved every moment. Lenny seemed to like it too. "Bravo! Bravo! *Squawk!*" he cried as the closing song played. Ellie giggled. She had taught Lenny to say "Bravo!" when she sang, which she did a lot. Now he said it whenever he heard any music.

"Did people really send telegrams back then?" Ellie wanted to know.

Nana Gloria nodded. "Oh, yes," she said. "Way before cell phones and e-mail, people sent them all the time."

"Nana, have *you* ever gotten a *singing* telegram?" Ellie asked.

"I have!" Nana Gloria replied with a smile. "I'll never forget it. Your grandfather sent me one for

my birthday once. It was one of the best presents I've ever gotten."

Ellie giggled. "It sounds like such a fun way to show your love . . ." She trailed off. An idea was quickly forming in her head: herself, Ellie, plus singing, plus delivering messages of love and friendship. It all added up to . . . singing telegrams for Valentine's Day! *That's something I'd do just for fun!* Ellie thought. *But maybe people would make a small donation to Puppy Love to have their message delivered. Then it would be for a good cause, too!*

Now if only she could just get Liz, Marion, and Amy to go along with the idea. . . .

# Chapter 3

# Singers for Hire

"I can't believe we're doing this," Amy said nervously.

"Ellie, are you sure we're ready?" Liz asked.

"Yeah," added Marion. "Maybe we need a few more practices?"

The girls were backstage in the school auditorium. In front of the curtain, the whole school was filing in for Monday morning assembly.

Ellie pulled her friends into a little huddle. "You guys," she said excitedly, "this is a great way to advertise our singing telegram service."

The day before, Sunday, Ellie had invited the girls over. She had explained her idea to raise money for Puppy Love. They had all agreed it was a great idea. Liz had even made some posters to hang up at school.

♡♪ Show Your ♡ Love ♡
Singing Telegram Service
♪♪ for Valentine's Day! ♪♪
$5 each, profits go to Puppy Love

Just tell us who the telegram is for and what kind of message you'd like to send. We'll write a one-of-a-kind song just for them and deliver it by Valentine's Day!

There was just one thing they didn't agree on. "Tell us again," said Marion. "Why can't *you* deliver the singing telegrams on your *own*?"

"You're such a great singer," Liz told Ellie.

"And so good onstage," added Amy. "Some of us . . . aren't."

Ellie beamed. She was enjoying her friends' nice words. But she also knew she and her friends would sound better all together.

"Come on," Ellie said. "It'll be fun

to sing together. And won't it feel more special for the person who is getting the telegram?"

Amy shrugged. Liz nodded. Marion smiled a tiny smile.

156

"Okay, then," said Ellie. "Let's do this!"

She peeked around the curtain. They just needed to wait for the sign from the principal, Mrs. Young. Ellie had worked everything out with her. Mrs. Young had only one rule: The girls couldn't deliver the singing telegrams during school hours. But she let them hang up the posters all around school. There was also a drop box in the hallway for telegram order forms and money.

Mrs. Young was announcing them. "Students," she was saying, "first up, we have a special treat. Four of our second-grade students are helping to raise money for a great charity called Puppy Love. They will be delivering singing telegrams for Valentine's Day!"

Mrs. Young waved to Ellie.

"That's our sign," whispered Ellie. She led the girls out onto the stage. Ellie took her place front and center. Liz, Marion, and Amy lined up behind her.

And then they began to sing, just as they'd practiced.

L-O-V, add an E,

That spells LOVE and love is free.

But for just five dollars, you can send

A musical note to your best friend!

Tell us who, tell us where,

Tell us when and we'll be there.

Tell us what to say, we'll turn it into song,

Show your love, you won't go wrong!

Ellie beamed as she sang. Her friends' voices blended beautifully behind her. For Ellie, it was over all too soon. The audience was clapping, and the girls were walking offstage. *I knew we should have*

*practiced a third verse,* she thought.

After the assembly, the four friends walked to their classroom together. "That was so great!" Ellie said excitedly.

"I don't know," said Amy uncertainly. "I messed up at least twice."

"I didn't even notice," said Liz, putting an arm around Amy.

"Me neither," said Marion. "I actually think we *did* sound good. Delivering singing telegrams could be really fun . . . *if* anyone signs up, that is."

DONATIONS
GO TO ♡
♡ ♡ PUPPY LOVE

At lunchtime that day, the girls walked past the drop box in the hallway. Ellie couldn't resist. She peeked under the lid.

"Well?" said Liz at her side. "Are there any orders?"

Ellie looked up, her eyes wide. She lifted the lid. The box was already half full! More than twenty people had already signed up to send a singing telegram!

Amy gasped, very surprised. Marion's jaw dropped.

Ellie clapped. "And we're just getting started!" she exclaimed. "Girls, we are in business!"

# Chapter 4

# Special Deliveries!

After school, the girls met up at Marion's house. They had a lot of work to do!

"Today is Monday," said Marion. She had her clipboard out. She started making a list. "We could start delivering telegrams tomorrow after school. Let's say we deliver about five a day. We can get them

all done by Friday afternoon—
Valentine's Day."

"We might get more orders!"
Ellie pointed out.

Liz nodded. "We'll have to fit
them in somehow," she said.

The group agreed to meet up
every day after school that week.

Then they got started on some tele-grams to be delivered the next day.

Amy loved writing poems, so she wrote the words to the song.

Marion decided on the tune of the music. She stuck to easy tunes, like "Happy Birthday" and "Row, Row, Row Your Boat."

Liz decorated a copy of the lyrics. The girls would give it to the person who received the telegram—as a Valentine's Day card.

Then Ellie led the girls in a rehearsal. They practiced singing each telegram a few times.

Soon they had ten singing telegrams, all ready to go. They took a break and had some hot cocoa.

"I can't wait to see the look on

the first person's face!" Ellie said
eagerly. "What a fun surprise!"

On Tuesday after school Dr. Purvis
dropped the girls off at the first
address. She had offered to drive
them from place to place. She

waited in the car while the girls went up to the front door.

"Everybody ready?" asked Ellie as she rang the doorbell.

Liz, Amy, and Marion nodded. They huddled around the lyric sheet. Within moments a dark-haired fifth grader opened the door.

"Hi!" said Ellie. "You're Rosie, right?"

The girl nodded.

"Then this is for you!" cried Ellie.

All together the girls started to sing.

Telegram For You!

Ro, Ro, Rosie Cho
from my soccer team,
I hope you have a
great Valentine's Day!
From your friend,
Eileen

Rosie clapped and smiled. "Oh, that's soooo nice!" she said. "Thank you!"

Then Liz handed her the lyric-sheet valentine. "Happy Valentine's Day!" she said.

And just like that, the girls had delivered their first singing tele-gram. They walked together down Rosie's front walk.

"Wow," said Amy. "That was kind of fun!"

"Did you see how happy she was?" said Liz.

"Where to next?" asked Ellie eagerly.

Marion checked her clipboard. Off they went to the next address, a block away. The second telegram was for a first-grade teacher from her students. It was a valentine *and* get-well message.

Telegram For You!

Mrs. West, Mrs. West,
Your foot really needs
a rest.
While you're out,
we'll try our very best
on this Friday's
spelling test.
From, Your Students

"Wonderful!" Mrs. West cheered. "You girls are fantastic! And so are my first graders."

The girls were on a roll. They delivered three more telegrams.

Then Marion checked her watch. "How about one more for today?" she said.

The others agreed. Dr. Purvis drove them to the last house of the day. Ellie rang the doorbell. A woman Nana Gloria's age answered the door.

"Hello!" said Ellie. "We have a singing telegram for Grandma Sue. It's from your grandchildren!"

Telegram for You!

We love you, Grandma Sue.
We know you've been feeling blue.
We'll help you
decide what to do
to cheer up your
Princess Boo.

The girls finished their song. Unlike the others, Grandma Sue did not clap. She did not smile. She didn't say anything.

She started to cry.

Ellie looked at her friends. A terrible thought flashed through her mind. *Oh no. Did we really sound that bad?*

# Ellie Meets a Princess

"That was lovely," Grandma Sue said at last, wiping her tears. "Thank you so much." She sniffed. "I'm sorry about all my crying. I've just been so very worried about my princess, that's all."

"Your princess?" Ellie said.

"Yes, my Princess Boo," said Grandma Sue. "She's my pet

lovebird. She's not well."

*"Awww,"* the girls said in unison.

Grandma Sue nodded. She explained that Princess Boo had seemed off lately. She wasn't eating much. Grandma Sue feared she was getting sick.

Ellie and the other girls looked
at one another. *A sick animal?* Ellie
thought. *Sounds like our thing!*

Ellie spoke up. "Amy's mom is a
veterinarian," she said. "Would you
like her to take a look at Princess
Boo right now?"

Grandma Sue's eyes went wide. "Oh, would she?" she asked.

Amy nodded. "I'm sure she would be happy to!" she said.

The girls were right. Dr. Purvis was more than happy to help. Within minutes, she was giving Princess Boo a quick checkup in Grandma Sue's living room. The girls and Grandma Sue looked on.

Princess Boo was a beautiful green bird with some pink and red around her beak and on her neck, and a bit of blue on her tail.

"Well, Dr. Purvis?" Grandma Sue

189

asked after a bit. "What's wrong with my princess?"

Dr. Purvis put Princess Boo back on her perch. "Nothing," she said. "At least, not medically. But I have

some questions. Does anyone else live with you, besides Princess Boo?"

Grandma Sue shook her head. "No, it's just the two of us."

"And how much of the day are you home?" Dr. Purvis asked.

Grandma Sue thought it over. "Well, I have a part-time job on weekdays," she said. "Three evenings a week I go to my book club. On weekends, I do errands. Sometimes I go on long walks with my friend. Otherwise I'm home. Why do you ask?"

Dr. Purvis nodded. "I think I know what's wrong," she said. "Princess Boo

might have a case of . . . loneliness."

"*Loneliness?*" said the girls and Grandma Sue all together.

Dr. Purvis explained that most lovebirds needed companionship. She said they were happiest when someone could be with them much of the day. "Some lovebird owners

have *two* of them," she said. "That way the birds keep each other company."

"Oh!" cried Grandma Sue. Her face brightened. "So I should get another bird!"

"Well," Dr. Purvis said, "first, I have an idea. Maybe Princess Boo could spend time with someone else's bird. See how it goes. If it seems to help her feel better"—Dr. Purvis smiled—"then you'll know if it's a good idea to get another bird."

Grandma Sue nodded. "That's a smart idea," she said. "There's just one problem. I don't know anyone else who has a bird."

Ellie felt her friends' eyes on her. She was already way ahead of them.

"I do!" Ellie cried.

# Bird Buddies

Liz, Amy, and Marion had just arrived at Ellie's house. It was Wednesday after school. The girls were going to write a few more telegrams. Then they'd head out to deliver some, too.

"I think Princess Boo is looking better already!" said Liz with a smile.

Princess Boo was inside her cage, which was right next to Lenny's perch.

"Grandma Sue dropped her off this morning," Ellie said. "She'll pick her up after dinner tonight."

Amy giggled. "It will be like a bird playdate!"

"Yep!" Ellie replied. "And I think she'll come again tomorrow.

Nana Gloria said they got along very well all day today."

"Very well! Very well!" squawked Lenny.

"See?" Ellie said, laughing with her friends.

The girls started on the telegrams. As usual, Amy got to work writing the words. Marion checked the address list. Liz sharpened her colored pencils.

Ellie had nothing to do until they were ready to practice. She let her mind wander. She thought about the people they had surprised the day before. They were all so happy! *It must feel great to get such a special surprise. I wish someone would send me a telegram!* she thought. She imagined it: the doorbell ringing, the surprise of seeing the girls there, singing a special song just for her.

*Who would it be from? A secret admirer? A friend? And what would the message be?*

"I was just thinking," Ellie said out loud to her friends. "What if someone wanted to send one of *us* a telegram?"

Amy looked up from her notebook. "One of us?" she asked.

Ellie nodded. "Yeah. Like, let's say, me. Just for example. How would that work?"

Liz smiled. "Hmm," she said. "You mean, how would we keep it secret? If the telegram were for you?"

"Right," said Ellie. "So that it would be a surprise for me. Or for any one of us."

Marion tapped her pencil eraser against her chin. "I'm sure we could figure something out," she said with a sneaky smile. "Why do you ask, Ellie?"

"Oh . . . uh!" said Ellie, "no reason." *No way*

*am I going to ask them to send me a telegram,* she thought. *That wouldn't be the same as someone sending it on their own.*

Ellie was quiet for a minute. Then she asked, "So no one has . . . ordered a telegram . . . for any of us?"

Marion shook her head. "Nope," she said. "Not yet."

# Chapter 7

# Lenny the Chatterbox

By Thursday afternoon the girls were getting a little bit tired. Meeting each day after school took up a lot of time.

And Ellie still had to squeeze in her chores—like walking their dog. Sam, their golden retriever, loved long strolls. But Ellie's friends were back at her house, writing

telegrams. She wanted to get back.

"Come on, Sam," she said. "Can we walk a little faster?"

But Sam wouldn't head home the short way. He pulled at the leash until Ellie let him walk on.

They went all the way around the block.

By the time they got home, the girls were putting on their coats.

"We're finished!" said Amy. "Everything's ready for tomorrow!"

Ellie was confused. "But . . . don't we have some to deliver?" she asked.

"Nope," said Liz. "The only ones left are the telegrams that people want delivered tomorrow— on Valentine's Day."

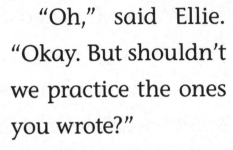

"Oh," said Ellie. "Okay. But shouldn't we practice the ones you wrote?"

"We did!" said Marion. "And you're so good at singing, you hardly need practice." She patted Ellie on the back. "I have to get home to do my homework."

"Me too," said Amy.

"Me three," said Liz. "Bye, Ellie!"

In a flash they were out the front door and gone.

Ellie stood frozen to her spot. "Well, they left in a hurry," she remarked.

Ellie took off Sam's leash. Then she went in to see Lenny. Next to him, Princess Boo was squawking cheerfully in her cage.

"I missed all the fun!" Ellie said to the birds.

"All the fun! *Squawk!*" said Lenny.

Ellie sighed. She flopped onto the sofa. "It's all Sam's fault. He sure was taking his time."

"Taking his time! Taking his time!" Lenny squawked. Then all of a sudden, he added: "Ellie's favorite song! Favorite song!"

Ellie looked up at him. "What?" she said.

"What? *Squawk!* What?" Lenny echoed.

Ellie stood up and walked over

to Lenny's perch. "No, before that. Did you say 'Ellie's favorite song'?"

"Ellie's favorite song! *Squawk!*"

"Yes! Yes!" Ellie cried. "You *did*! But . . . why?"

Ellie knew that parrots like Lenny could mimic. That meant they could copy words or sounds they heard. "But I didn't say those words," said Ellie. "You must have heard them from someone else."

"Someone else! *Squawk!*" Lenny screeched.

Then it hit her. *The girls!* she thought. *The girls were just in here. They were working on telegrams.*

*Why would they be talking about my favorite song?*

Everyone knew Ellie's favorite song was "Take Me Out to the Ball Game." Ellie's family loved going to baseball games. She dreamed of singing that song at a big-league game someday.

*But why would the girls talk about that while writing telegrams?* Ellie wondered.

There was only one explanation that made sense to her.

*I'm getting a telegram tomorrow!*

# Chapter 8

# Ready, Set, Surprise!

Ellie looked in the mirror. She practiced her happy, surprised face. *Perfect!* she thought. *I don't want to look like I was expecting a telegram.*

She checked her outfit: her red wrap sweater, red skirt with sequins, and pink leggings.

Ellie felt ready for Valentine's Day. And she was *definitely* ready to be surprised!

*I just wonder* when *they'll deliver my telegram,* she thought on her walk to school.

Their teacher, Mrs. Sienna, had planned their classroom party for the morning. Everyone in class had a valentine mailbox—a decorated paper bag taped to each desk. The kids walked around the classroom to deliver their valentines.

Liz, Marion, and Amy came up to Ellie.

"Ellie," said Marion with a big smile, "we have something for you."

*This is it!* thought Ellie. *They're going to deliver my singing telegram now. How exciting!*

Liz was reaching into her backpack. "We all worked on it together,"
she said.

"We hope you like it," added
Marion.

Ellie got ready to flash her happy,
surprised face. Liz handed her a
heart-shaped card.

Ellie looked at it quickly, then up at her friends, expecting the singing to begin.

But it didn't. Liz, Marion, and Amy just stood there smiling.

That's when Ellie realized: It was just a valentine—not a singing telegram.

"Oh!" said Ellie. She tried hard not to look disappointed. "What an awesome valentine. You guys are so sweet.

WE LOVE you, ELLIE! Liz, Marion and Amy

Thank you all so much!"

Ellie told herself they were just saving the telegram for later. *Mrs. Young* did *say no telegrams at school*, she thought.

The girls met up after school at Marion's house. Marion checked

her clipboard. She had the list of addresses they would be going to. "So," said Marion, "there's one very important telegram I think we should deliver first."

Ellie's eyes went wide. *Does she mean my telegram?*

"That's right!" said Amy. Ellie

thought she had a twinkle in her eye. "Ellie, you weren't there yesterday when we talked about this special one."

"Oh? Which one?" Ellie asked. She tried to act natural. But inside she was jumping up and down. *Mine! They must mean mine!*

"Ellie, you're going to love this!" said Liz.

*I know! I am going to love it!* Ellie thought.

Liz went on. "We are delivering another telegram to Grandma Sue—from us this time."

"To give her the good news!" Marion added. "You know, that Princess Boo seems one hundred percent better!"

"My mom agrees," says Amy. "She thinks getting another bird

should do the trick."

Ellie forced a huge smile. "That is a great idea!" she said.

And she *did* think it was a great idea. She was so happy Princess Boo was better. But Ellie couldn't help feeling a pang of jealousy. Grandma Sue was going to get *two* singing telegrams?

Still, Ellie tried to be patient. *Sooner or later, I'll be getting my telegram,* she thought. *Won't I?*

The girls grabbed their coats and the telegrams. Marion led the way toward the garage. Mrs. Ballard

had offered to drive them.

Marion stopped at the garage door. "Oh! I almost forgot," she said. "We're going to sing Grandma Sue's telegram to the tune of 'Take Me Out to the Ballgame.' It seemed to fit well with Amy's words. Plus, we knew you'd know it!"

"It's your favorite song, isn't it?" said Amy.

Ellie nodded while her heart slowly sank. So the girls *had* been talking about her favorite song. But they had been writing a telegram for Grandma Sue—not for her.

"Yes," Ellie said distractedly, as if in a daze. "I do love that song."

But right at that moment, Ellie didn't feel much in the mood to sing it.

# The Last Telegram

"Ta-da!" said Ellie's mom. She put a plate down in the middle of the dining room table. On it were five chocolate-frosted cupcakes with Valentine's Day decorations on top. "Something sweet for my valentines!" said Mrs. Mitchell.

"Yum!" cried Ellie's brother, Toby, reaching for one.

"Thanks, Mom," Ellie added with a little smile as she took one.

Ellie took a bite. The cupcake was so yummy. But Ellie was still feeling blue. She and the girls had had a busy afternoon of delivering telegrams. Delivering Grandma Sue's was especially fun. But now dinner was over and Valentine's Day was almost over too.

*Oh, well,* she thought. *No singing telegram for me.* Ellie didn't know why she cared so much. She guessed she just wanted to feel special. She tried to cheer herself up by remembering she had done a great thing for Puppy Love.

Ellie was helping her dad clear the dishes when the doorbell rang. She went to answer it.

"Hi, Ellie!" Liz, Marion, and Amy were standing on her front porch. All three were wearing huge grins.

"Hi, you guys," Ellie replied uncertainly. "What's up?"

"Well," said Liz, "we have something for you!"

With that, the three girls started to sing to the tune of "Take Me Out to the Ball Game."

For Ellie ♥
First you had a great idea.
Then you had a great plan.
We weren't so sure about
singing at school.
You helped us through it
and it turned out cool,
and now Puppy Love pups are smiling.
They want to say something too!
For it's one, two, three,
and they'll
bark out a big
THANK-YOU!

By the end, Ellie was clapping
while jumping up and down.
"Wow!" she exclaimed. "That
was the best! The absolute best!"
She hugged each one of them.
"You three are the best friends in

the whole wide world!"

Marion laughed. "Thanks, Ellie!" she said. "We're glad you liked it!"

"But the telegram isn't from us, you know," Amy added.

Ellie stared. "It's not?"

"Nope," said Liz. She handed Ellie the heart-shaped telegram. On the back, there was a PS.

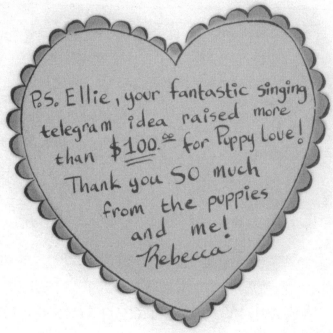

P.S. Ellie, your fantastic singing telegram idea raised more than $\underline{\$100.^{\infty}}$ for Puppy Love! Thank you SO much from the puppies and me!
— Rebecca

"We raised more than *a hundred dollars*?" cried Ellie. "That's so cool!"

"Yeah, and that's not all," said
Amy. She handed Ellie something
in a frame.

"Wow! We can hang this at the
Critter Club!" Ellie said excitedly.

"And just think of all the puppies that will be helped with the

money we raised—from your idea!" said Liz.

Marion put an arm around Ellie. "We were going to deliver your telegram earlier," she said. "But Rebecca wanted to sign the valentine herself."

Liz smiled. "We were sort of getting the feeling that you'd enjoy a telegram of your own."

Ellie pretended to be confused. "What in the world gave you that idea?" she said. Then she laughed and her friends joined in.

Ellie wasn't sure what was the best: getting a singing telegram, truly helping Puppy Love, or having three best friends who knew her so well.

Suddenly, it felt like the sweetest Valentine's Day ever.

241

# the CRitter club

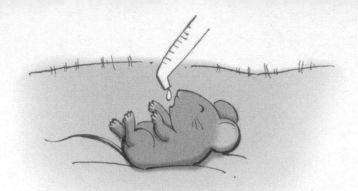

# Table of Contents

# Sleepover at the Lake!

*Squee-onk! Squee-onk!* A loud, shrill sound woke Liz Jenkins. *My alarm clock sounds broken,* she thought, only half-awake.

Liz rolled over in bed and rubbed her eyes. No, it wasn't her alarm clock. It was a goose honking! Sunlight shone in through the window. Birds chirped outside. It was going to be a beautiful spring day at the cabin.

Liz threw off her flannel sheets and jumped out of bed. "Yes!" she cheered. "It's the perfect weather for the girls' visit!"

Liz's three best friends, Ellie, Marion, and Amy, were coming up to the Jenkins' lake cabin *today* for the three-day weekend. For years, they had heard all about it from Liz. She and her family had been coming to Marigold Lake since Liz was little. But this was the first time Liz had been able to invite her friends.

Liz hurried to change into her clothes. She had lots of things to get ready before the girls arrived. She

wanted their first visit to the lake to be perfect.

Out in the cabin's living room, Liz's mom, dad, and big brother, Stewart, were already up. Her dad was making breakfast. Her mom

was sweeping up pine needles from the floor. Stewart was setting the table.

"Oatmeal in ten minutes, Lizzie!" her dad said.

"Thanks, Dad," Liz replied. She was headed for the door. "I'll be back. I just need to do a few things."

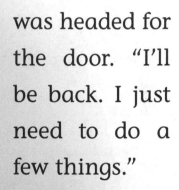

Outside, Liz took a deep breath. *Ahhhh.* Fresh air. She

smiled at the sight of the big, beautiful lake in the cabin's backyard.

Liz went into the storage shed. She dragged a folded-up tent to a flat area by the campfire pit. "Just the spot," Liz said out loud to herself. She would ask her mom or dad to help her set up the tent later. It

was definitely warm enough for the girls to sleep outside in it. Liz couldn't wait to surprise them!

Next, Liz hurried down to the boat dock. She took the tarp off the red canoe and made sure the life jackets were there. *We can paddle around the whole lake,* she thought.

Then, on her way back to the cabin, Liz picked up every long, thin stick she saw. *We're* definitely *roasting marshmallows over a campfire*, she decided. She left her pile of roasting sticks next to the campfire pit.

Liz stopped to think. Canoeing, swimming, camping out, marshmallow-roasting, plus hiking on the nature path . . .

*I hope we have time for everything!* she thought excitedly.

Back inside the cabin, Liz joined

her family at the table. They had already served her oatmeal and yogurt—their usual super-healthy breakfast. Her dad passed her some berries to sprinkle on top while Liz told them about her preparations.

Liz's parents smiled. "Sounds like you've thought of everything," her mom said.

Then Stewart added, "But won't you guys just be painting your nails and stuff? Or whatever you do at your sleepovers?"

Liz rolled her eyes at her brother.

"*Actually*, my friends are so excited to have a wilderness weekend. I told them about all the animals up here—the rabbits, squirrels, deer, and foxes."

Liz and her friends were different in lots of ways, but they all shared one thing: a love of animals. Together they ran an animal shelter called The Critter Club in their town of Santa Vista. They helped all kinds of stray and hurt animals.

"You told them about *all* the animals we've seen?" Stewart asked. "Like the snakes? And the bear we saw that one time?"

Liz hadn't exactly mentioned *those*. Her friends weren't as excited as Liz was about unusual animals. Like the cool pet tarantula they

took care of at The Critter Club over the summer. Ellie, Marion, and

Amy were glad Liz wanted to be in charge of it.

Liz shrugged and ate her oatmeal. *My friends will love the lake as much as I do!* she thought. *Or almost as much. Or at least they'll like it a lot.*

# Welcome to the Wilderness!

Ellie's mom's van pulled up to the cabin just after lunchtime.

"Liz!" Ellie cried, jumping out of the back of the van. "Oh, we have missed you!"

Amy and Marion jumped out behind her. Marion giggled. "We just saw her *yesterday* at school," she reminded Ellie.

"I know!" said Ellie. "But so much has happened since then."

Liz and her family had driven to the lake the day before—on Friday afternoon. So Liz had missed the girls' after-school duties at The Critter Club.

"Don't worry, Liz," Marion said. "We'll get you all caught up."

The four girls huddled for a group hug. "I'm so glad you're here!" Liz told them. "Now the fun can begin!"

They said goodbye to Ellie's mom. Then Liz led her friends

down to the lake. They sat on the boat dock. There the girls told Liz the latest Critter Club news.

"First of all," said Amy, "our stray isn't a stray anymore."

Liz gasped. The girls had been taking care of a stray cat for a few weeks. "She's been adopted?" Liz asked.

"Even better," said Ellie. "Her owner called! He saw the ad you drew for the newspaper, Liz. Oh I brought a copy."

Liz's family didn't get the paper at their cabin, so she was excited to see her art in print.

Stray Cat Found!
Gray female with
white patches.
Sweet, gentle, very healthy

Can you give her a home?
Call The Critter Club!

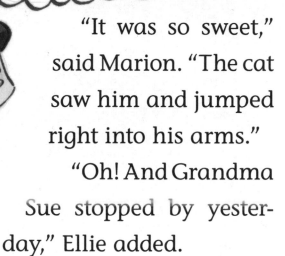

"It was so sweet," said Marion. "The cat saw him and jumped right into his arms."

"Oh! And Grandma Sue stopped by yesterday," Ellie added.

Grandma Sue wasn't Ellie's grandmother. The girls just called her that. They had met her when they delivered a singing telegram to her from her grandchildren.

"She came with her new love-bird, Princess Two," Ellie went on. "Princess Two and Princess Boo are already best friends."

The girls had helped Grandma Sue when Princess Boo was acting

strangely. With the help of Amy's mom, a veterinarian, they figured out the bird wasn't sick—she was just lonely. That's why Grandma Sue had gotten a second bird.

"Oh, I'm sad I missed the chance to meet her," Liz said. But she shook off her disappointment. Her friends were here and they had the whole weekend ahead of them. "Let me show you guys around."

The other girls jumped up, ready to follow their tour guide.

Liz took them to the cabin. She pointed out the solar panels up on the roof. "All of our hot water is heated by the sun," Liz said.

She showed them the outdoor shower. "You can rinse off here after

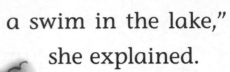

a swim in the lake," she explained.

Liz took them inside. She showed them the shelves full of books and board games next to the fireplace.

Finally, Liz showed the girls her room.

"This is so great, Liz!" Ellie exclaimed.

"Yeah," said Amy. "No wonder you love it up here."

Marion was looking around Liz's room. "I *love* your room," she said.

"But there's only one bed in here. Where will *we* sleep?"

Liz's eyes lit up. "I'm glad you asked," she said. "Follow me."

Liz led the way back down

toward the lake. She stopped next to the campfire pit. "Ta-da!" she said, presenting the tent. Her dad had already set it up for them. "We can sleep here tonight. Won't that be the best?"

Liz looked at her friends' faces. Amy looked kind of excited. Ellie looked curious.

Marion looked worried. She glanced at Liz. She glanced at the tent. Then she glanced at Liz again. "You mean we're going to sleep . . . *outside*?" she said.

# Shivers and Jitters

"Last one to the floating platform is a rotten egg!" Liz shouted. She dove off the boat dock into the lake. She swam toward the platform. When she came up for air, she looked around.

Where were her friends?

Liz looked back at the boat dock. Marion was shivering, wrapped in

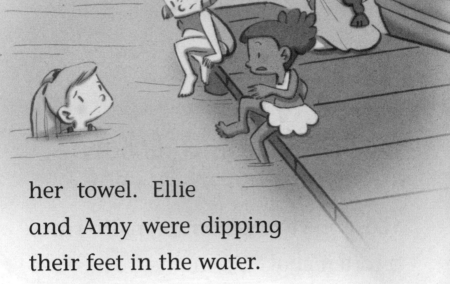

her towel. Ellie
and Amy were dipping
their feet in the water.

Ellie called out to Liz: "It's kind
of cold, isn't it?"

"Not really!" Liz called back.
"Just jump! It's great once you're in
the lake!"

But the girls didn't look so sure.
So Liz swam back to them.

Liz climbed out onto the boat dock. "I have an idea," she said to them. "Let's hold hands. On the count of three, we all jump in together. Okay?"

The girls looked at each other. One by one, they each nodded.

"One, two, three . . ."

They all jumped in with a *splash*!
When her head popped up, Amy
squealed loudly: "Eeeeeeek!"

"It's freeeeeeeeezing!" exclaimed
Ellie, half-laughing.

"Ohhmygosh, ohhmygosh," said
Marion, treading water.

"Keep swimming! Follow me!"

called Liz. "You'll warm up. I promise!"

The girls played Marco Polo and swimming tag. Soon they were having a blast. They floated on their backs and looked for pictures in the clouds. They talked while blowing bubbles in the water, seeing if each other could understand.

They were all laughing when they climbed onto the floating platform in the middle of the lake. The sun-warmed wooden planks felt nice as the girls stretched out to rest.

Then the breeze picked up. Before long, Marion, Ellie, and Amy were shivering.

"I think I'm r-r-ready to go in," Marion said. Her teeth chattered.

"Oh," said Liz, "okay." She had hoped they could spend a while doing silly jumps off the platform. But she didn't want her friends to be cold. So they swam back to shore.

Back on land, the girls changed into dry clothes. Liz's dad offered to take them on a nature walk.

"We can collect cool leaves," Liz suggested. "Then I'll show you how to make some fun leaf prints."

Ellie smiled. "Nature plus art," she said. "Sounds like Liz, all right!"

The girls laughed as they followed Liz's dad toward the nature trail. Stewart waved from the cabin porch. "Have fun! Watch out for snakes!" he called.

Ellie stopped in her tracks. *"Snakes?"* she said, her eyes wide with fear. "What snakes?"

# A Very Short Walk

It took a while for Liz and her dad to reassure Ellie.

"We've never seen any *poisonous* snakes," Liz pointed out.

"That's right," said Mr. Jenkins. "And in *all* the years we've come to the lake, we've only seen a few snakes total."

Liz could tell Ellie wasn't so into

the nature walk anymore. But Ellie finally agreed to come along. "I want to walk in the middle of the group—not up front, not in the back," she said.

The nature trail went all the way around the lake. It was a walk that usually took Liz about an hour.

Just ten minutes down the trail, Liz, Marion, and Amy already had handfuls of leaves. Ellie was too busy watching for snakes to look for leaves.

"Here's my favorite so far," said Liz, holding up an oak leaf.

"I like this one!" said Amy.

"Oooh, birch!" said Liz. She knew a thing or two about the trees around the lake.

Marion held one up. "How about this one?" she asked

"Maple, for sure, Liz replied. "So pretty!"

Ellie sighed. "Oh,

I'm being ridiculous!" she said. "I want to find a special leaf too." She took one step off the trail, reaching down for a leaf. Her foot came down on the very end of a long stick. The other end popped up from underneath a pile of leaves.

Ellie jumped up and screamed. "Aaaaaaah! Snaaaaaaaaake!" She took off, running back toward the cabin.

Liz's heart sank. Poor Ellie! It seemed the nature walk was over.

291

# Chapter 5

# Row, Row, Row Your Boat

Back at the cabin, Stewart was very sorry when he saw how upset Ellie was. After all, he was the one who had put the idea of snakes in her head. To make it up to the girls, he offered to take them on a canoe ride. "I'll row the row boat," Stewart said. "You guys ride in the canoe. We can tie the two together and I'll tow you around the lake."

Ellie cheered up right away. "That sounds fun!" she said, beaming at Stewart. "But could I ride with *you*?"

Stewart shrugged. "If you want," he said.

The five of them put on life

jackets. Then Stewart tied a rope line from the back of the row boat to the front of the canoe.

Soon Stewart was rowing them out into the middle of the lake. In

the canoe, Marion, Amy, and Liz lounged and relaxed.

"I could get used to this," Marion said.

"Me too," said Liz. "Stewart has never, *ever* rowed me around the lake before."

The late-afternoon sun was getting low in the sky. The water on the lake was still, except for the pools made by Stewart's oars. Liz sighed. It was a peaceful, happy, perfect moment.

Just then, on the far side of the

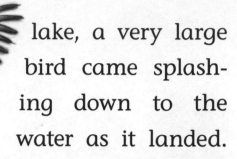 lake, a very large bird came splashing down to the water as it landed. Amy gasped. "Wow!" she cried. "Is that a great blue heron?" She leaped to her feet, straining to see.

"Wait!" cried Liz. "Don't stand—"

It was too late. Amy teetered, then lost her balance. She fell out of the canoe, her foot catching the side. The whole canoe flipped, dumping Marion and Liz too.

When Liz came up from under the water, the first thing she heard

was Stewart laughing. But Liz didn't mind. She started laughing too. Liz had lost track of the number of times she and Stewart had tipped the canoe over the years.

Marion started giggling too. "Good thing I brought an extra pair of shoes!" she said.

"Are you guys okay?" Ellie called from the row boat. Liz could tell Ellie was trying not to laugh at her wet friends.

The only one who did not look amused was Amy. Liz recognized the familiar flush of pink on her cheeks.

Amy was completely embarrassed.

# Chapter 6

# The Campout

Inside the cozy cabin, a warm fire crackled in the fireplace. Liz sat at the table, watching her family and friends chatting happily. Her parents had made them all a big dinner.

But Liz was feeling blue—and not very hungry. She loved grilled tofu and beet salad and roasted organic sweet potatoes. But did her mom have to make it this weekend? *Couldn't we have spaghetti, or something I know my friends like?* she thought.

Ellie was mostly pushing the tofu around on her plate. Marion hadn't touched the beets. Amy was chewing slowly and taking lots of sips of water.

After dinner, the girls settled into

the tent. Their four sleeping bags fit inside perfectly. Liz's mom found extra flashlights so each of them could have one. Then she zipped the tent flap closed.

"Good night, girls," she said through the nylon. "Don't stay up too late."

In the flashlight glow, the girls crawled into their sleeping bags.

"Marion," said Ellie, "did you bring your notebook?"

"Of course!" Marion replied, pulling it out of her backpack. Marion was super organized. She

loved making lists, so she always had paper and a pen.

"Great!" Ellie exclaimed. "We can play Two Truths and a Lie."

"Oh yeah," Amy said. "That game we played last weekend at our sleepover!"

The girls took turns hosting a sleepover nearly every Friday night, so they knew a lot of sleepover games. To play Two Truths and a Lie, each girl got a slip of paper. She wrote down two things about

herself that were true and one that was not. Then the others had to figure out which one was the lie.

Liz stared at her paper, thinking. Then she wrote:

I love grilled tofu.

I once swam all the way across the lake.

Then she added:

I am having a bad weekend.

The last one should have been a lie, but it was actually the truth. Liz knew Marion didn't even want to sleep out here. Poor Ellie was freaked out by the snake-stick. And Amy was still embarrassed about tipping the canoe. Plus the lake was too cold for them, and the food was too weird.

Liz sighed. She crossed out her last sentence and tried to think of a different one—one that really *was* a lie.

## Some Squeaky Guests

*Everything looks a little brighter with the sun,* Liz thought the next morning. That's what her mom always said. She unzipped the tent flap and peeked outside. It was a new day. Liz was ready to leave yesterday's troubles behind.

"Sleeping out here was so fun!" Amy said. They were walking up to

the cabin for breakfast.

"Yeah!" said Ellie. "Can we do it again tonight?"

Liz nodded. She noticed Marion wasn't saying anything, but she tried not to worry about it.

On the porch, they passed the leaf prints they had made the day before.

"They're dry," Liz announced.

"They look so good!" Marion said, holding hers up.

"They really do," Amy agreed.

"Liz," said Ellie, "you've made us all artists!"

Liz smiled a huge smile. The prints *had* turned out beautifully. More important, her friends had fun making them. Maybe Ellie's snake-stick scare had been worth it after all.

Inside, the girls found Liz's parents huddled over a cardboard box on the kitchen counter.

"Oh girls," Mrs. Jenkins said, "are we glad you're here!"

Liz and her friends looked at one another, puzzled. "What's going on?" Liz asked.

"Well," Mr. Jenkins explained, "last night we heard some noises."

Liz's mom nodded. "Little tiny squeaks. Coming from somewhere inside the cabin. And this morning, we found what was making them."

She nodded toward the box. The girls came over to look inside—and gasped.

"Awwwwww," Liz cooed.

"They're adorable!" cried Ellie.

Cuddled together on a kitchen towel at the bottom of the box were a bunch of tiny animals. They were covered in a light brown fuzz. They

319

had long, skinny, pink tails and rounded ears. Their eyes were shut tight.

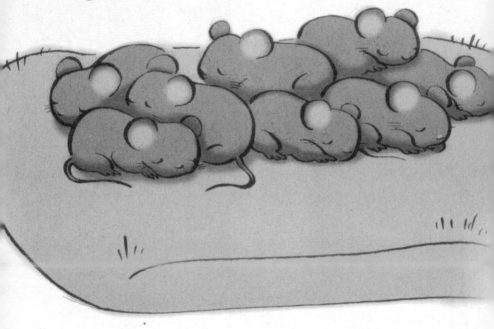

"Baby mice?" Amy asked.

Liz's dad nodded. "Yep! We found them in the back corner of

the pantry closet. There was a little nest too. But we can't find any sign of the mother."

"They looked so cold in there," Liz's mom added. "We thought they might be more comfortable in this box. There's a hot water bottle under the towel to keep them warm."

"What if the mother comes back?" Amy asked. "She won't be able to find them."

"Oh, no! She'll be so worried!" Ellie said dramatically.

The girls thought for a minute. Liz's eyes lit up. "I have an idea!" she cried.

Liz got some scissors from a kitchen drawer. Carefully, she cut out a mouse-size hole on one side of the cardboard box. "A door for Mama Mouse," she explained.

Then Liz carried the box to the

pantry closet. She laid it gently in the back corner. "Now they're snug and comfy, but if their mom comes back, she can find them."

Liz's friends and parents agreed: it was the perfect solution. Liz felt very proud!

"There's just one more thing," said Ellie. "What if the mother *doesn't* come back?"

# Critter Sitters

The girls knew one person who was sure to have some answers: Amy's mom, Dr. Melanie Purvis.

Amy used the cabin phone to call her mom back in Santa Vista. Marion sat next to her. She took notes in her notebook to help Amy remember everything her mom told them.

"So?" said Ellie the moment Amy hung up the phone. "What did your mom say?"

Amy sat down in front of the fireplace. The girls gathered around, eager to hear all the info.

"Mom thinks they're probably about two weeks old," Amy said.

"And what did she say about the mother mouse?" Liz asked.

"Well," said Amy, "here's the bad news: she said if it's been more than a couple of hours, the mother probably isn't coming back."

Liz, Marion, and Ellie looked

at one another, not knowing what they could do.

"But there's good news," Amy said. "We can take care of them. They'll need our help to eat for a few weeks."

Huge grins spread across the girls' faces.

"The Critter Club's work is never done!" Liz exclaimed.

Marion showed them her notes. She had made a list of supplies they needed to take care of the mice.

Kitten or puppy formula
(replacement milk)

Eyedropper

Water bottle
(like for a hamster)

Liz's dad offered to go shopping. "There's a pet supply store in town," he said. "I'll run out and get what you need."

"In the meantime," Liz's mom said, "why don't you girls head down to the lake? I packed you a picnic breakfast." She held up a basket filled with muffins and fruit. "And I'll keep my eye on the mice for you."

The girls thanked Liz's parents. Liz took the basket and led the way down to the boat dock.

"So what should we do today?" Liz asked the girls as they nibbled on blueberry oat bran muffins. "There's a cool waterfall in the woods I could take you to."

Ellie frowned. "In the woods?" she asked. "How far into the woods?"

Liz sighed. *Oh right,* she thought. *Ellie's still nervous about the snakes.*

"Ah-CHOO!" Marion sneezed a huge sneeze. "Bless you!" Liz, Ellie, and Amy said all together.

Marion sniffled. "Thank y—ah-CHOOOO!" She sneezed even louder and rubbed her eyes. "Uh-oh."

"What's the matter?" Liz asked.

"I just hope I'm not getting sick," Marion replied. "You know, from the chilly lake yesterday. I have a horse show next week that I do *not* want to miss. Maybe I'd better not swim today."

Marion rode her horse, Coco,

in all kinds of competitions. Sometimes they even won ribbons. Liz hated to think the trip to the lake had made Marion sick.

"And I guess I'd better stay out of the canoe," Amy said. "I don't want to dunk anyone again!" She said it with a half laugh. But Liz wondered if Amy still felt bad about the whole thing.

Liz turned her head away from the girls. She stared out at the lake. Her vision was getting blurry as her eyes filled with tears. She bit her lip, trying hard not to cry.

*They hate it here*, Liz thought.

*Swimming is out. Canoeing is out. Hiking to the waterfall is out.*

"Should we just take the baby mice and head back to Santa Vista today—a day early?" Liz asked them.

With the words out, she couldn't hold back the sobs anymore. Liz covered her face, turned, and ran off the boat dock.

# Chapter 9

# Friends to the Rescue

"Can we come up?" Ellie asked.

She, Marion, and Amy craned their necks, looking up at Liz. She was in a tree, about ten feet off the ground.

Liz nodded. "Yeah, sure." She sniffed. She wiped her eyes. She'd let it all out. Now she was feeling better— although maybe a little silly.

"Actually," Ellie called up, "can you come down?"

Liz looked down. The girls were having trouble climbing the tree. She couldn't help laughing through her sniffles. She had forgotten that

it took her one whole summer to figure out how to get up into that tree!

With a few quick moves, Liz was
back on the ground. "I'm sorry, you
guys," she said. "I just . . . I just had
all these ideas about how this weekend would be. I wanted you to have

a great time. I guess I didn't realize how much I wanted it."

Her friends moved in. They all wrapped their arms around Liz. Liz put her head on Ellie's shoulder.

"You don't have to say sorry for

being sad," Ellie said. "We're your best friends!"

"She's right," said Amy. "Friends should be honest about their feelings."

Marion nodded. "So we'll be honest," she said. "We *are* having a great time."

Liz looked up at them. "You are?" she asked. *"Really?"*

All three of them smiled and nodded. "Really!" they said together.

"But . . . but . . . ," Liz began.

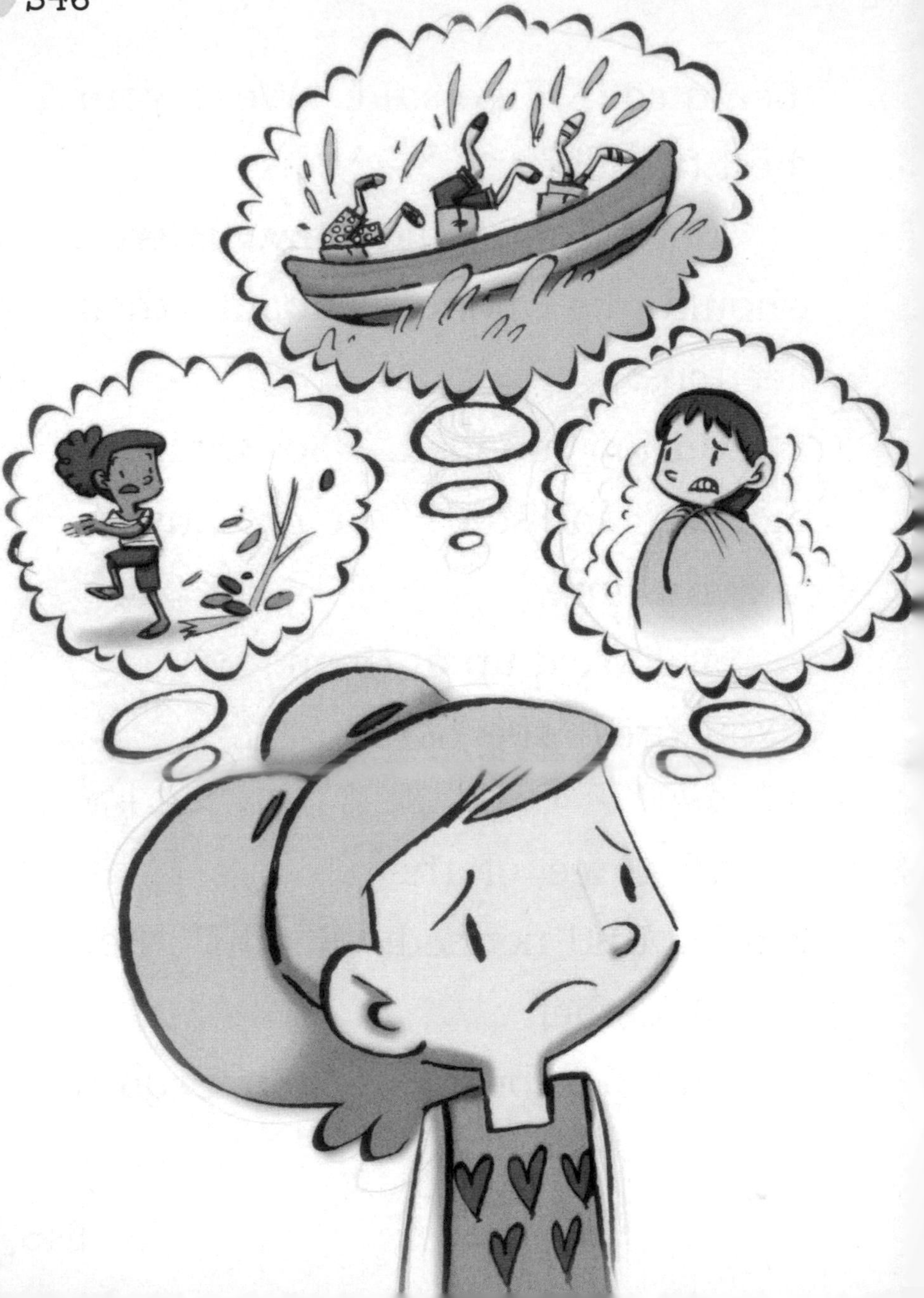

She listed all the things that hadn't gone as planned: the snake-stick, the flipped canoe, the water that was too cold for them. "Nobody feels like swimming or canoeing," she added. "And now Marion might be getting sick."

Marion gave Liz a squeeze. "Oh, don't worry about that," she said. "I'll be fine. I just need to eat more of your mom's veggies, I guess."

"And yesterday was *so fun*!" said Amy. "We had a blast swimming—before we got chilly. Even canoe-ing was great." She giggled. "I can actually laugh about it now."

Ellie chimed in. "It makes a good story, that's for sure," she said. "And I know there's no reason to be afraid of a little snake. I'm in The Critter Club, after all!"

Ellie stood up straight and tall.

"So it's decided," she went on. "You're taking us to that waterfall. The one deep, deep in the woods. The deeper, the better!"

The girls laughed together.

"Aw, thanks, you guys," Liz said. "I feel so much better. You really are the best friends in the world."

"You too, Liz," said Marion. "And you're the world's best wilderness guide. So lead the way!"

# Chapter 10

# Campfire Chat

That night, around a glowing campfire, the girls roasted marshmallows with the sticks Liz had collected. Liz turned her stick slowly so her marshmallow cooked evenly all around.

Then, as they ate their treats, they talked about the day.

"My favorite part was the

waterfall, for sure," said Ellie. "I'm so glad I braved the evil snake-stick to see it."

"Well, my favorite was canoeing," Amy said. "I didn't even flip it *one time* today."

Marion put another marshmallow on her stick. "I think my favorite part of the day is still to come," she said. "You're not going to believe it: it's sleeping outside in the tent!"

*"Really?"* the girls said.

Marion nodded. "I've never done it before this weekend," she explained. "But I really like it. Being

354

out in the cool air, bundled up in a cozy warm sleeping bag, plus the sound of the crickets all around . . . It's the best!"

Liz gave a happy little clap. "Well, that does it," she said. "I think *this* is my favorite part." Hearing what her friends loved about the lake made her day. Then she had another thought. "This *and* taking care of the mice. They are just so cute. And they need us so much."

The mother mouse had not returned. So every few hours that day, the girls had fed the babies,

with the help of Liz's parents. They used the
special milk Liz's
dad bought at the
pet supply store.
They dripped drops

of it into the babies' tiny mouths.

"My mom says we have a tough decision ahead," Amy said. "After we bring them to The Critter Club, when the baby mice are bigger, they could be released back into the wild. They are wild animals, after all. Or we could try to find homes

for them as pets."

Liz wasn't sure what the right thing to do was. "If we let them go, would they be okay?" she asked.

Amy shrugged. "It's hard to say," she said. "We would need to help them get ready. My mom says there's a special kind of mouse

house we could build for them. It would help them get used to living outside on their own."

Liz stared into the campfire. The flames jumped and danced. "It's funny," Liz said. "Tomorrow our wilderness weekend is over. But it turns out we'll be taking some of the wilderness home with us!"

It sounded like The Critter Club girls were going to have their hands full with the mice for a little while. Liz knew they'd figure out the right thing to do—together.

"So . . . , " Liz said slowly, "do you guys want to do another trip to the lake sometime?"

"*Yes!*" Ellie, Marion, and Amy all replied at the same time—and Liz knew they really meant it.

# the CRItteR club

## Marion Strikes a Pose

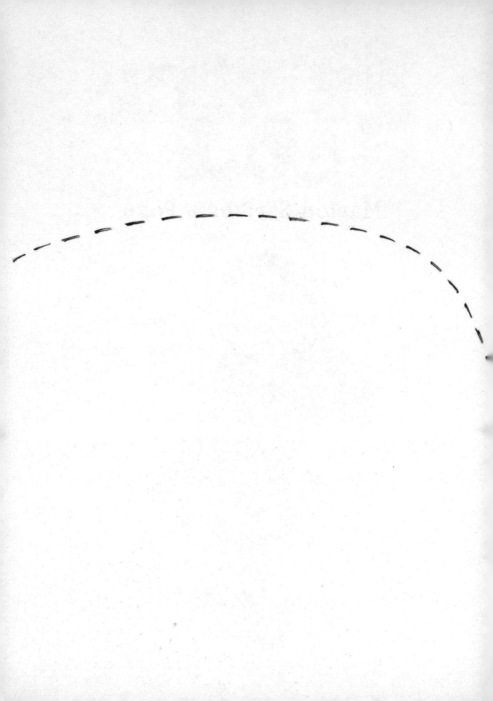

# Table of Contents

# Ready, Set, Style!

Marion walked in the front door of Santa Vista Elementary School. In her head, she was going through her morning checklist: *Homework folder? Check. Lunch box? Check. Sneakers for gym? Check.*

Marion felt ready for the day.

She followed other kids into the auditorium for the morning

assembly, which they had every Friday. The seats were filling up. Marion headed for the rows assigned to the second-grade classes. She spotted an empty seat next to her three best friends, Amy, Liz, and Ellie.

Walking toward that row, Marion passed a group of fourth

graders. "I love your skirt, Marion!" said a girl named Emily as Marion went by.

"Thanks!" Marion replied. She had spent a lot of time last night planning her outfit for today. She added one more item to her checklist. *Cool outfit? Check!* Marion loved picking out her outfits for

school. And for play dates and for parties. And for riding her horse, Coco. For everything, really!

"Hi, Marion!" said Amy as she sat down. Farther down the row, Ellie and Liz waved.

"Attention, students!" Mrs. Young,

the principal, spoke into the microphone at the front of the auditorium. All the kids quieted down. "I have some announcements. But first, we have a special guest. Her name is Hannah Lewis. She is the owner of The Closet, a store here in Santa Vista."

The students clapped.

Marion gasped. *The Closet!* It was her absolute favorite clothing store.

Marion sat up straight in her seat as Hannah Lewis walked up to the microphone. Marion loved Hannah's outfit— an extra-long top with a leather belt, black leggings, and ballet flats. Plus she had on some cool beaded necklaces.

"Good morning, everyone," said Hannah. "Thank you, Mrs. Young, for letting me come today. I want to announce that we will be having a special fashion show at The Closet in a few weeks."

*A fashion show*, Marion thought. *How fun!*

"The purpose of the show is to raise money for a charity," said

Hannah. "It provides free clothing to children who need it, so it's a very good cause. We hope the fashion show will get lots of people to come shopping at our store that day. All the money we earn will go to the charity."

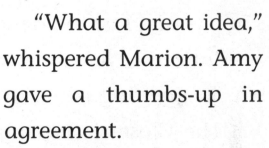

"What a great idea," whispered Marion. Amy gave a thumbs-up in agreement.

"But I need *your* help,"

Hannah went on. "Our store is a *kids'* clothing store. And I was thinking: Who knows best what kids like to wear? Kids! So I am looking for some young fashion designers."

Marion's eyes went wide. This was just getting better and better!

"The Closet is having a styling contest," Hannah explained. "To enter, you style an outfit—head to toe. I will pick one winning look from each grade. Those will be the outfits in our fashion show!"

Now Marion was so excited she could hardly sit still!

"Contest entries are due a week from Monday," Hannah went on. "I have flyers here with all the rules. If you are interested, please come up to get one."

Marion jumped out of her seat, ready to get a flyer.

Seeing Marion, Hannah laughed. "*After* assembly," she added. "But I like your enthusiasm."

Marion sat back down, too excited to even be embarrassed. She felt as if this contest had been made just for her.

*I have to win!* she thought. *I just have to!*

# Froggy Fashion Show

After school, the girls met at The Critter Club. That was the animal shelter they had started in their friend Ms. Sullivan's empty barn. At the club, they took care of stray and hurt animals and tried to find homes for them.

They also did a lot of pet sitting. Right now at The Critter Club they

were taking care of some frogs for a family that was on vacation. It was Liz and Marion's turn to check on the frogs, but Amy and Ellie had come, too. It was fun to all be there together.

Always organized, Marion pulled the frog feeding schedule

from her backpack. "I guess it's my day to feed them," she said. "But, do you want to do it, Liz?"

"Yes!" Liz cried excitedly. For Liz, the more unusual the animal, the better. Turtles, snakes, spiders—she loved them all.

Marion shivered. The frogs were not exactly *her* favorite Critter Club guests. They looked so slimy. And they ate bugs. Yuck!

While Liz fed the frogs, Marion pulled the contest flyer out of her backpack. She hadn't stopped thinking about it since assembly.

The Closet's Styling Contest!

Style a head-to-toe outfit for a girl or boy.

Use your own clothes or come "shop" at The Closet to borrow clothes for your outfit design!

"Are you going to enter?" Marion asked her friends.

Amy shook her head no. "Maybe if it was a writing contest," she said with a smile.

Liz also shook her head. "I don't know how to *design* an outfit. Mine just kind of happen."

"What about you, Ellie?" Marion asked. Ellie loved dressing up. Ellie twirled around and then curtsied. "I'd rather be *on* the stage than styling *back*stage." she replied.

The girls all laughed. That was Ellie, all right! She loved being in the spotlight.

"Well, I have a favor to ask of you guys," Marion said. "I stopped

at home and picked out an outfit for each of you from my closet.
You know, to get my styling ideas
started."

Marion pulled out the clothes
she'd brought. "I thought we could
play Fashion Show. Right here in
the barn!"

Marion had brought a sparkly skirt and satin blouse for Ellie.

"Cuuuuute!" Ellie cooed. She rushed into a storage room to try them on. She was back in less than a minute.

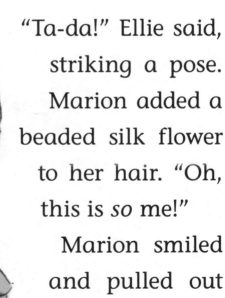

"Ta-da!" Ellie said, striking a pose. Marion added a beaded silk flower to her hair. "Oh, this is *so* me!"

Marion smiled and pulled out Amy's outfit. It

was a striped yellow T-shirt dress.

"Would you try it on?" Marion asked Amy. *"Please?"*

Amy didn't look so sure about the fashion show idea, but she agreed. She went off to change and came back, all smiles.

"This is *definitely* something I would wear," Amy said.

Finally, Marion had a colorful outfit for Liz: a bright green dress and rainbow-striped leggings.

Liz had just taken the lid off the frog tank to feed the frogs, but she

glanced over. When she saw the outfit, she clapped happily. "I can't wait to try that on! You really know our styles!"

"Thanks, Liz." Marion said. "That's so nice to—EEEEEK!"

Marion shrieked as a frog jumped out of the tank.

The frog landed on the table.

"I'll get it!" said Amy. "Oh, wait! We're not supposed to touch them." Amy grabbed a butterfly net. She tried to catch the frog but it quickly hopped away. "Hey, come back here!" she cried.

The frog hopped onto the outfit Marion had brought for Liz.

"Shoo! Shoo!" Marion cried. The slimy frog was hopping all over the clothes! "Somebody get it off!"

Finally, Amy scooped up the frog in the net. She gently put it back into the frog tank. Marion took a deep breath. Liz, Amy, and Ellie turned to look at her.

Then all four girls burst out laughing.

"You know, Marion," said Liz, "frogs are really cool in lots of ways."

Amy nodded. "My mom is going to come next week. She can teach us more about them."

Amy's mom, Dr. Melanie Purvis, was a veterinarian. She often helped the girls care for the animals at The

Critter Club. "Who knows? Maybe you'll even learn to like them."

Marion smiled and didn't say anything. *I wouldn't count on that!* she thought.

# A Wrinkle in the Plan

"What a great idea!" said Liz. She was looking at the stack of cards Marion had made over the weekend. Each one had a photo of an item of clothing Marion owned.

"I call them style cards," Marion said as Liz handed them back. "I can carry them around and flip through them to get design ideas."

It was Monday and their class was in the art room. Liz and Marion sat across from each other at one end of a long table. Today they were painting with watercolors.

Marion had carefully painted a few lines, but most of her paper was empty. She didn't love painting.

Paintbrushes didn't have erasers. What if she messed up?

Next to Marion, a girl named Olivia leaned over. "Marion," she said, "could *I* look at those?" She pointed at the stack of style cards.

"Sure!" Marion replied. She handed the cards to Olivia.

Olivia studied them carefully, looking very interested. "You always wear the coolest outfits," she told Marion.

Marion smiled. "Thanks!" she exclaimed.

Olivia nodded and went back to flipping through the cards.

Marion was surprised by the compliment. She had never really noticed Olivia's taste in clothes before. Today Olivia was wearing a purple sweater with a crooked heart on it, black jeans, and purple high-top sneakers. It seemed like their styles were really different.

Olivia passed the cards back. "Thanks for letting me

look," she said, and gave Marion a friendly smile. Marion smiled back.

"Could I ask you a favor?" Olivia asked her.

Marion nodded. "Sure."

"Well, I was wondering . . ." Olivia began. She looked unsure of her words. "Could you maybe, I

don't know, give *me* some fashion tips sometime?"

Marion was so flattered. She and Olivia were friendly, but they didn't know each other super well. *She must* really *like my fashion sense to ask me for advice*, Marion thought.

Marion smiled. "Sure!" she told Olivia.

"Thanks!" Olivia exclaimed happily. "Maybe now I'll have a shot at winning."

Marion was confused. "Winning?" she asked.

Olivia nodded.
"Winning the styl-
ing contest," Olivia explained. "I'm
entering, too."

"Oh." It was all Marion could
think of to say. But her mind was
racing. She and Olivia were both
in second grade. Hannah would
choose only one winning look from

each grade. So if Olivia was entering, and Marion was entering, that
meant . . .

Olivia was her competition.

And Marion had just agreed to
help her win.

# Style School

Marion laughed, looking down at her Saturday breakfast. Her mom had made it look like a mouse in a sleeping bag. The mouse had a banana-slice head, chocolate-chip eyes, and two blueberry ears. The sleeping bag was a folded pancake. There was even a pillow—a toast rectangle—under the mouse's head.

Marion hurried to finish her breakfast before Olivia came over. The girls were getting to be good friends. Already Olivia had been over three times that week.

At first Marion wasn't sure about helping Olivia. But she quickly changed her mind. After all, she was just giving Olivia fashion tips—not styling her outfit *for* her.

So on Tuesday, Olivia came over after school. Together the girls played mix-and-match design with all of Marion's style cards.

"Don't be afraid to mix patterns and fabrics," Marion advised. "A denim jacket looks great with a silky striped skirt."

On Wednesday, the girls played dress-up with Marion's party clothes. Olivia didn't even mind that Gabby, Marion's little sister, wanted to play, too. She had a little

brother about the same age.

"Make sure *you* like your outfit," Marion said, sharing another tip. "Clothes look better if you feel good wearing them."

On Thursday, the two of them talked about accessories: scarves, belts, and shoes.

"You know, one fun accessory can make a whole outfit better!" Marion pointed out.

Marion liked getting to know Olivia. Olivia was really nice. She liked animals. And she cared about the charity that The Closet was raising money for. Olivia reminded Marion that the contest wasn't all about winning; it was also about helping people.

By Saturday, Marion not only really liked Olivia, she also wanted Olivia to do well in the contest.

It was a nice day, so the girls sat out on Marion's back porch. They sipped lemonade through curly straws.

"Okay, here it is," said Marion. "This is my big fashion tip. Pick one part of your design— either the shoes, or the pants, or the

top, or an accessory. Pick one part
and do something . . . unexpected!
Make it unique."

Olivia nodded. "That makes

sense," she said. "So, nothing *too* crazy. But something that will make our outfits stand out in the contest." She pulled her curly straw out of her glass. "Like this straw," she said with a giggle. "You could use it in an outfit as a—"

"Cool hair accessory!" Marion suggested.

Olivia's jaw dropped. "That's what I was going to say!"

Marion laughed. "Great minds think alike," she said.

# Frog Facts

Later that afternoon, Marion was outside The Critter Club playing fetch with Ms. Sullivan's dog, Rufus. She threw a stick across Ms. Sullivan's backyard. "Go get it!" she said.

Rufus bounded after the stick. He was getting so big! Marion could remember when she'd first met Rufus. He'd gotten lost one day and the girls helped Ms. Sullivan find him.

Rufus brought the stick back. He dropped it at Marion's feet. It was covered in doggy slobber.

"Ew, Rufus," Marion said with a laugh.

"Ma-ri-on!" Amy called from the barn door. "My mom's here."

Amy's mom had come to teach the girls more about frogs. Ellie and Liz were already inside.

Marion gave Rufus a good-bye pat and headed for the barn.

Dr. Purvis was standing by the frog tank. Ellie, Liz, and Amy were gathered around.

"Hi, Marion," Dr. Purvis said. "I

want to show you girls how to clean out the frog tank. But first, how about I share some of my favorite frog facts?"

"Okay!" said the girls together.

"Here's one," said Dr. Purvis. "You know how we call a group of birds a *flock*? Well, we call a group of frogs . . . an *army*."

The girls laughed.

"An army of frogs," said Marion. "Oh no. I'm getting a picture in my mind. It's totally terrifying!"

"Wait," said Amy. "Listen to this one. Mom, tell them the one about the skin."

Dr. Purvis smiled. "Yes, well, most frogs shed their skin about once a week."

Liz looked puzzled. "Once a week?" she said. "But we've had these frogs for a week." She looked into the frog tank. "Why aren't there any old frog skins anywhere?"

"Good question, Liz," Dr. Purvis said. "You don't see the old skins because the frogs *eat* them."

"Coooool!" said Liz.

"Whoa," said Ellie.

"Yikes!" said Marion. They ate bugs *and* their own skin? She was mostly grossed out. But one part of it was cool: The frogs weren't letting anything go to waste.

"I have a question," said Ellie. "Why can't we touch them?"

"Because frog skin is thin and sensitive," Dr. Purvis explained. "It's designed to let in air and water—and whatever else it touches. Even right after we wash our hands, we still usually have stuff on them—like oils or soap residue. If we touch the frogs, then those things could get inside

the frog's body and make it sick. That wouldn't be good."

*Hmm. That is pretty interesting,* Marion thought. She leaned down and peered into the tank. One of the frogs seemed to be staring back at her.

She pretended the frog could read her mind. *I don't want to pick you up,* she thought. *And you don't want me to pick you up.*

Somehow, knowing that made Marion like the frogs better. It was like they understood one another.

# Decisions, Decisions

The big day had come.

Shopping day!

Marion's mom had driven her to The Closet so she could borrow clothing, as the flyer said. She was picking out the actual clothes that would make up her outfit. Then, at school tomorrow, she would meet with Hannah to present the outfit.

"I'll be right over there, looking at shoes for Gabby," Marion's mom said. "Call me if you need me."

Marion was happy to browse on her own. In fact, she was in heaven. Marion looked down at her notebook. It was open to her outfit sketch.

She was most proud of the scarf idea she'd had. She was hoping to find an extra-large patterned scarf at The Closet. She wanted to tie it over her basic pieces. It would be an unexpected touch!

Already, Marion had found a simple blue skirt and a matching top. They were perfect for the base layer. "Now where are the scarves?" Marion wondered.

Looking around for a salesperson to ask, she passed the fitting rooms. One of the doors opened. Out stepped . . . Olivia!

"Marion!" she cried.

"Hi, Olivia!" said Marion. "It's so funny that we're here at the same time." She looked down at what Olivia had on: a denim jacket with ruffles, a flowing green skirt, tights, and low brown boots. "Is this your design?" Marion asked. "I love it! It looks great!"

Olivia scrunched up her face.

"Really?" she said. "I'm not sure about it. Actually, I have another one in here. I think it's better than this one." Olivia's face brightened. "Can I show you? You can tell me which one *you* like better."

"Okay!" Marion replied.

Olivia went back into the fitting room. Meanwhile, Marion scanned the racks. She spotted some scarves on a shelf and headed over to check them out.

Behind her, Marion heard the fitting-room door open and then Olivia's voice. "So what do you think of this one?"

Marion turned. Her eyes took in Olivia's outfit, head to toe. Marion felt something like a knot twisting in her stomach.

Olivia was wearing slim purple pants and a sleeveless shirt. Over the top, tied to look like a dress, she had on *an extra-large flower print scarf.*

Marion could not believe it! Olivia's scarf looked like it had come straight out of Marion's notebook.

Marion thought the outfit was amazing. She *loved* it. She opened her mouth to say so. But she didn't want to say so. Because if that was Olivia's design, what would Marion do? Their outfits couldn't be so similar!

"It's nice," Marion said. "But you know what? The first outfit was better. I'd go with that other one."

As soon as the words were out of her mouth, Marion wished she could take them back.

# A Strange Feeling

*In the school auditorium, Marion was showing her outfit design to Hannah. She struggled to get the scarf tied the right way. Each knot she made just came untied.*

*Marion looked up. In the back of the auditorium, Olivia stood in the door-way. She pointed at Marion's scarf. "There it is!" Olivia cried. "Get it!"*

Olivia stepped aside, and Marion saw it: an army of huge frogs. They were hopping two by two down the auditorium aisle. They were headed right for Marion!

Marion woke with a start.

Morning sunlight shone through her curtains. She sighed with relief. It was just a dream. A terrible, terrible dream.

But as Marion rubbed her eyes, a certain feeling in her stomach came back. What was it? Then Marion realized—she felt guilty. She had lied and convinced Olivia to choose the first outfit.

Then, after Olivia had left the store, Marion had gone ahead with her design. She had chosen the blue

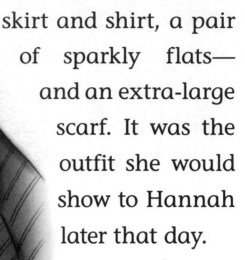

skirt and shirt, a pair of sparkly flats— and an extra-large scarf. It was the outfit she would show to Hannah later that day.

*At least I didn't get the exact same scarf Olivia picked out,* Marion thought, trying to make it seem less terrible. *Is it really such a big deal?*

But deep down, Marion knew it was. She had lied because she

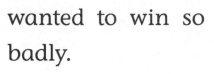

wanted to win so badly.

Marion jumped out of bed. She had to get to school and find Olivia. She had to tell her the truth.

The Closet

# chapter 8

# Marion Makes It Work

The clock outside the auditorium read 3:42. School was dismissed. The buses were gone. The pickup circle was empty.

The only students left at school were the ones who wanted to enter the styling contest. There were three other second graders, plus about ten kids from other grades.

But Olivia wasn't there. She hadn't been in school at all that day, so Marion hadn't had a chance to talk to her.

Marion was next in line to have her meeting with Hannah.

*What am I going to do?* Marion

The Close

wondered. Her heart beat faster. In a shopping bag, she had the clothes from The Closet. But Marion didn't feel good about them. *I want to win. But then, what if I do win? I won't feel proud or excited.*

The auditorium door opened. Hannah poked her head out and called, "Next!" She looked at Marion with a smile.

Marion took a deep breath as she walked in through the door.

At the foot of the stage, there was a mannequin the size of Marion. "Your name is Marion Ballard?" Hannah asked as she checked her clipboard. "And you're in second grade?"

Marion nodded.

"Great," said Hannah. "So, why don't I help you dress this

mannequin with the outfit you've put together. Then I'll have a few questions for you. Okay?"

"Sure," said Marion. She pulled out the blue skirt and the blue shirt. Hannah helped her wriggle the clothes onto the mannequin.

Then Marion pulled out the scarf.

"And where does this fit into your design?" Hannah asked.

"That goes . . ." Marion began. She froze. She couldn't do it. She just couldn't use the scarf the way she—and Olivia—had pictured it. It didn't feel right.

But she had to use the scarf. Otherwise, her outfit was too plain.

Thinking quickly, Marion held one end of the scarf. She twirled it around until it was twisted up, long and thin.

She wrapped it around the mannequin's waist like a belt and tied it
in a large bow at the right hip.

Marion stepped back to look at
it. It wasn't as good as her original
scarf idea. But it wasn't bad.

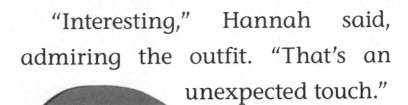

"Interesting," Hannah said, admiring the outfit. "That's an unexpected touch."

Marion smiled for the first time that day.

# The Moment of Truth

The rest of the meeting was a blur. Hannah asked Marion why she was entering the contest and a few other questions. Before Marion knew it, she was walking out of the auditorium.

As she opened the door, she saw Olivia waiting in line. "You're here!" Marion said. "But . . . where

have you been? Why weren't you in school today?"

Olivia wiped at her nose with a tissue. "My allergies were really bad this morning," she said. "My dad said I should stay home and rest." She held up a bag. "But I'm ready with my outfit. I can't wait for my turn to go in!"

Marion looked down at the floor. "Olivia, about your outfit," she began. This was going to be hard. Marion knew she had to tell Olivia the truth. "I lied to you yesterday. I said I liked your first outfit better, but really I *loved* your second outfit."

Olivia looked confused. "You did?" she asked.

Marion nodded and explained everything—how they had had the same scarf idea, and how

Marion hadn't wanted to change her design. "I should have told you. We could have talked it over." She looked Olivia in the eye. "I'm sorry."

Olivia smiled. "That's okay, Marion," she said. "Because you know what? I'm not going to use

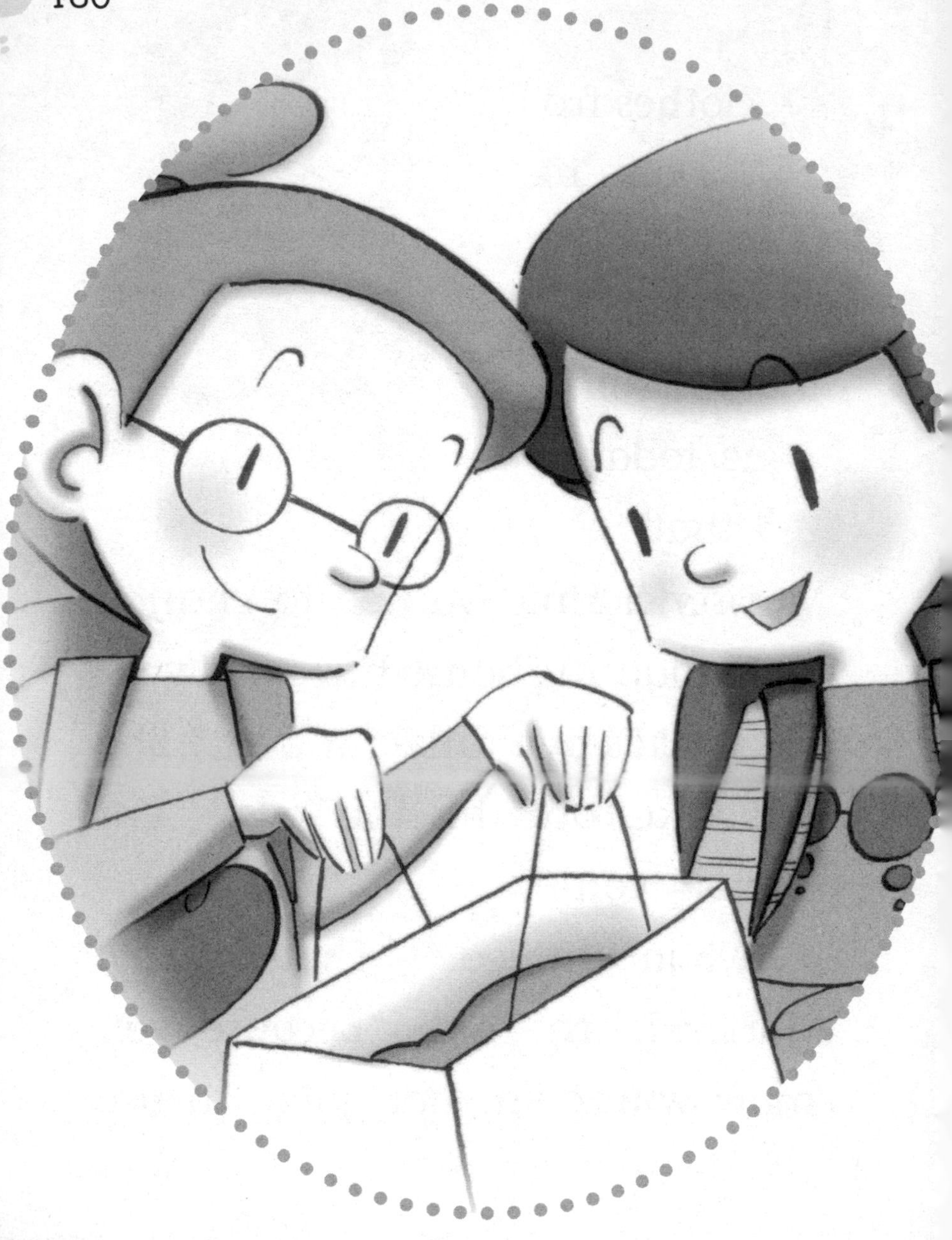

the clothes from The Closet."

Marion raised her eyebrows. "You're not?" she said.

Olivia shook her head. "See, I realized something when I was at home today," she started. "I realized that . . . I do kind of like my own style. I mean, I learned a lot from you, and your style is amazing. But it's just not mine."

Olivia opened her bag so Marion could peek in. "So this is my outfit: my high-top sneakers, a skirt that is so much fun to twirl around in, and my favorite

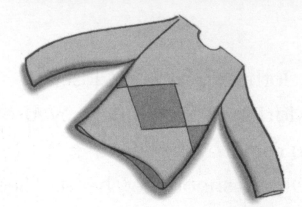

sweater. My grandma gave it to me. It's something I would feel good wearing."

Marion smiled a huge smile. "I love it!" she said. And she really meant it.

She waited in line with Olivia, then wished her good luck when Hannah called her in. "I'll wait out here until you're done," Marion said to Olivia.

Olivia nodded and gave her a thumbs-up as the auditorium door closed behind her.

# Showtime!

A week later, Marion ran full speed into The Critter Club. "Hello?" she called, out of breath.

No one answered. "Amy? Liz? Ellie?" she said. It was time to feed the frogs. But the other girls hadn't arrived yet.

In one hand, Marion clutched a piece of paper. At last it had come

in the mail: a letter from Hannah Lewis with the list of contest winners. Marion sat down by the frog tank to wait. She looked inside. One of the frogs hopped right up to the glass.

"Oh, hello," Marion said to the

frog. She looked down at the letter. She looked back at the frog. Then she shrugged. She was dying to share the news with *someone*.

She held the letter up to the glass. "Look!" she exclaimed. "Look who won in second grade!"

Second-Grade
Winners:
Olivia Warren
and Marion Ballard

The frog croaked.

"I know!" said Marion. "Isn't it great? I'm so excited!"

The frog didn't say anything else, so Marion went on. "I can't decide which is better. Winning, or winning *with* Olivia!"

There was no answer from the frog tank.

"And Hannah Lewis called me just now. She said she loved both of our designs. She said they were *both* so stylish and so different."

Marion was sure the frog was listening to every word she said.

"And here's maybe the best part: Hannah said if we want to, we can model our outfits in the fashion show! That's right. We can be *in* the show! Can you believe it?"

The frog was quiet. Marion

was all out of news. She sat for a
moment, just looking at the frog.
She leaned in closer to the glass.

"You know what?" whispered
Marion. "You are a very good

listener." She looked around. She felt a tiny bit silly talking to a frog. Then she added, "And you guys are *actually* pretty cool."

One week later, Marion was backstage at The Closet's fashion show. She peeked out at the audience from behind the curtain. The seats were filled and loud music played. Everyone clapped as the contest winners took turns walking the runway, showing off their outfit designs.

"Marion, you're next," Hannah

473

whispered behind her. "Ready . . . and go!"

Marion took a deep breath and stepped out onto the runway. She felt so proud to show off the outfit she had styled. She was even prouder of the hard decision she had made to

change her design. In the end, she loved the way the outfit turned out.

By the sound of the audience's applause, they liked it, too!

At the end of the narrow stage, Marion struck a pose. She could see her friends and family cheering loudly for her.

Marion turned and began her walk off stage. As she did, she passed Olivia on her way down the runway in her own winning outfit.

Marion put her hand up for a high five. The friends' hands met in the air with a loud clap.

Then, as Marion walked on, she smiled a huge smile, listening to the crowd cheer for her friend.

Read on for a sneak peek at the next Critter Club book:

 #9

# Amy's Very Merry Christmas

At her mom's vet clinic, Amy Purvis peeked into the guinea pigs' cage. She had just hung a new toy from its top. *Will they figure out how to play with it?* Amy wondered.

Snowy, the white guinea pig, tried it out first. He sniffed at the jingle bell dangling at the end of a silver velvet ribbon. *Jingle.* The bell

rang softly. Snowy darted away and hid inside a tissue box.

His brother, Alfie, came over next. He nudged the bell with his paw. *Jingle-jingle!*

Before long, the two guinea pigs were taking turns batting at the bell.

Amy smiled as she watched them play. "Happy holidays, guys!"

It was a week before Christmas. Snowy and Alfie had been staying at the vet clinic for a few days. Their owner had brought them in because they seemed sick.

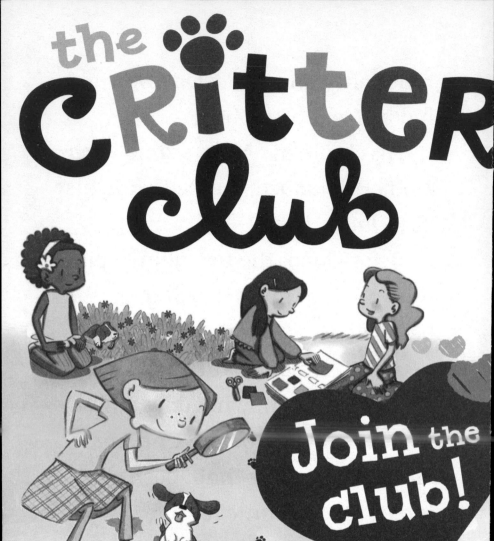

Join **the** club!

Visit CritterClubBooks.com for activitie
excerpts, and the series trailer!